C.P. Time

ORDER THIS BOOK FOR FRIENDS
AND FAMILY

www.beneaththeunderdog.com

JEAN-CLAUDE @ BENEATH THE
UNDERDOG.COM

Booklocker.com, Inc.
2003

C.P. Time

Jean-Claude Lewis

CHAPTER 1

*A single gunshot rang out. The sound, generated by a twelve-*speaker circumferial home theater system, startled Julian out of a deep sleep. He jerked and almost fell off the leather sofa, then sat up and looked around the room. His muscular shoulders sagged in relief to discover he was alone in his recreation room.

Julian's appearance did not agree with the image of his profession. He was one of the world's foremost scientists of nuclear and quantum physics. Most of Julian's peers had a rumpled appearance and needed haircuts. Julian had the face and body of a GQ model and a wardrobe to match. In even greater contrast to his appearance was his favorite hobby, the study of American and world history. The neatly displayed history books completely covering the entire rear wall of his recreation room served as evidence of that interest.

As he shrugged off his grogginess, he realized he had fallen asleep and accidentally changed the television channel on the huge panoramic screen that covered an entire wall and a third of each adjacent wall. Two smaller monitors, positioned below the panoramic screen were still tuned to the NFL special about the Detroit Lions, winner of Super Bowl XLI, some years back.

He yawned and brought his left hand to his mouth nearly hitting his bottom lip with the Membronic glove on his hand. The glove, recently available, was like a remote control device worn on the hand, but unlike a basic remote control, it could be programmed to respond to hand motion. It also responded to voice commands in any language, even if the wearer suffered from a speech impediment and could not speak clearly. He had completely forgotten he was wearing it.

Julian started to make the motion that would make the Membronic glove change the station back to the NFL special. But before he could move his hand, the program on the panoramic screen captured his attention. It was a special about the life and death of Dr. Martin Luther King, Jr.

James Earl Ray, Dr. King's assassin, had fired the gunshot that awakened Julian. The words to Dr. King's "I Have a Dream" speech played in the background and he wondered what the world would be like now, had Dr. King still been alive. Meanwhile, on the two smaller monitors, the football special was abruptly interrupted and replaced by a story of a surfaced American submarine and a Norwegian fishing vessel, apparently caught in a violent storm. The caption at the bottom of the monitors read, 'Channel 7 Action News: Live action footage from the North Sea via satellite.' Julian quickly tuned the panoramic monitor to Channel 7.

Sounds of the roaring sea filled the room. The powerful, pounding waves violently tossed the Norwegian fishing boat. He focused entirely on the events unfolding on the television screens.

*****

The USS *Finback* SSN-670, the "crackerjack" submarine of the east coast, was on its last mission prior to its decommission by the U.S. Navy. Although saddened by the Navy's decision to decommission her, the crew often heartily joked about how many razor blades would be made out of her HY-80 steel hull. The crew of the *Finback* knew razor blades weren't made from submarine steel but they had an affinity for the Gillette Mach 3 razors issued by the Navy. It was a ritual for the men to use them to shave their heads completely bald while submerged at sea for long deployments. They had actually renamed the razor the *Macho 3,* which seemed to fit the personality of submarine crewmembers. After all, it took *more* than a real man to go to sea and stay submerged for as long as six months at a time. 'Real mission—Real men' was the *USS Finback's* motto.

The crew was the best. Because of the intensity, and the interdependence of the crew of an American submarine, every sailor aboard had to understand how the entire submarine worked. They needed to be ready to perform anyone's job at a moment's notice. It didn't matter if a sailor were a nuclear engineer or a cook. Once he reported on board he had one year to learn the operation of every system on the boat. Only then, would he be awarded his shiny insignia, called 'Dolphins', that would be proudly worn on his uniform.

Top secret and dangerous missions that were slated as *one-way* and suicidal were given to the *Finback* whose crewmembers were required to update their wills before going to sea. Then, once the mission was underway, just after submerging, the captain recited the Lord's Prayer over the 1MC, the boat's public address system.

The USS *Finback* had won many Battle E awards for efficiency, and had made several North Sea runs during the Cold War in the mid-1980s. In fact, the submarine for which the *Finback* was named had rescued a young WWII fighter pilot named Captain Bush from the Pacific Ocean after the Japanese shot him down in 1943. Years later, this young pilot became President George Bush, the forty-first President of the United States and the father of George W. Bush, the forty-third President of the United States.

In 1987, the *Finback* was on a mission in the Arctic Sea, just off the coast of the Soviet Union. It was 0300 hours as the American submarine sat on the bottom of the sea, near the Russian shipyard at Murmansk. They had just finished installing video equipment on the floor of the sea when several active sonar pings sounded in the water. The sound reverberated throughout the entire ship. Everyone who was awake stopped what he was doing and looked up toward the surface of the water. Those who were sleeping awoke and did the same.

In less than fifteen seconds, Captain English climbed the ladder and entered the Control Room. Wearing only his pajamas, a slipper and a robe he had only managed to slip one arm through, he barked to the Officer of the Deck (O-O-D), "Report!"

The OOD, trying hard not to look unraveled, answered with a neutral expression, "It's a French destroyer, Sir. It's outside the twelve-mile limit and it's just pinging the water at random, not really looking for anyone."

Captain English responded, "If she just happens to find us with one of her *random pings,* it will alert any Russians who may be listening, we're here also."

The Russians would not hesitate to torpedo an American spy submarine. Everyone looked on during the tense moment. The next decisions by his captain would spell life or death for them. It took Captain English little time to come up with a solution.

"Load torpedo tubes one and four. If she pings us, blow that French piece of trash out of the water! While they're trying to sort out what's happening, get us the heck out of here. They can court martial me when we get back, but we're getting back," Captain English said, his face as hard and rigid as Mt. Rushmore. Fortunately for the *Finback,* and especially the French, the French destroyer never located the American submarine.

Now, years later, and on her last mission, the proud *Finback* was caught in a torrential rainstorm with hurricane force winds. Like a salmon trying to swim upstream, she struggled to surface near the sinking Norwegian fishing vessel.

The aft end of the Norwegian ship began to disappear beneath the sea like a miniature version of the Titanic. Some crewmen slid down the deck to cold, watery graves. Others frantically tossed lifeboats and life preservers overboard. The rainstorm and turbulent sea, however, had no mercy on the lifeboats.

Logically, it appeared as if resistance was futile and would only prolong the inevitable. But the desire to survive was stronger than logic, so the fishing crew followed their hearts and fought for life.

As the *Finback* surfaced, Petty Officer Satterfield, the lead diver, briefed the rescue divers at the Auxiliary Machinery Room 1 Hatch. To a casual observer it may have seemed that not one man on the team was listening to Satterfield. They labored fervently, checking and double-checking their diving gear, which included a blackened stainless steel knife, a diver's watch and a strobe light locator beacon attached to the shoulder of the diving suit.

Appearances were deceiving. The crew heard every word Satterfield spoke. Any missed instruction, word, or even voice inflection could result in loss of life. Satterfield had been a dedicated Navy man for over twelve years. He was in his early 30s and boasted wide, muscular shoulders that showed off his crackerjack Navy uniform to perfection. Most sailors referred to this uniform as a monkey suit. Whenever a fellow sailor alluded to Satterfield's monkey suit, Satterfield quipped in response, "I look good in a suit, any suit, except a prison suit."

Satterfield was a 'spit and polish' sailor. He had only one blemish on his otherwise exemplary military record. It resulted from an incident that had occurred early in his career. Since Satterfield loved red beans and rice and was from North Carolina, he was called Cornbread. In spite of the country nickname, he had a flair for style. His fire-orange convertible Triumph Spitfire was one testament to that.

When Satterfield sat in his Spitfire, a small, sporty convertible, he made the car look even smaller. As he drove around town it seemed as if he were driving a large, bright-orange shoe.

Just for fun, Satterfield's vanity license plate read 'Gigolo.' After all, who could afford a gigolo in the seedy part of Charleston, South Carolina, that Satterfield spent most of his time? *Someplace*

Else, his favorite local dance club, was in that part of town. One night a woman asked him if he was really a gigolo.

"How can I be?" he replied, "Y'all don't have any money."

Satterfield often remarked that the people in that section of Charleston were so poor when they parked illegally the police didn't put a boot on the car; they put a flip-flop on it.

His career setback happened the first month he was stationed in Charleston. Upon reporting to the *USS Thomas Jefferson SSN 618* he was briefed about the community, as is standard protocol for all new personnel reporting to a new command in the Navy. Besides normal community information, another topic was discussed.

"Stay away from Geechy women!" the briefing officer warned. "They make up a sizable part of the local population. They look and sound like people from the Caribbean Islands and they have been rumored to practice voodoo. But, never, I repeat, never, eat red beans and rice cooked by a Geechy woman!"

Although Satterfield appeared to be paying close attention to the lecture, his mind was racing away on ten different subjects, the most important subject being which dance club he would visit that evening. But the mention of red beans and rice got his attention. He quickly raised his hand, and when recognized, asked, "Why not, Sir?"

The briefing officer paused, measuring his answer before he spoke. "Of course, the Navy can't take an official position on this. But we do know a lot of sailors who have been eating the red beans and rice have gone U.A., unauthorized absence. These sailors are usually missing for months before we find them. When we do find them, they're usually hiding out at some Geechy girlfriend's house."

"We can't confirm it," he continued, "But we think they put some sort of voodoo in the red beans and rice. The bottom line is, if the Navy would have wanted you to have a girlfriend they would have issued you one in your seabag."

The briefing officer added, "But it's a funny thing. They can only make the special red beans and rice for one week every month. And don't ask me what they put in the red beans and rice. As I said, the Navy will take no official position on this."

Ending that subject, the briefing officer winked his right eye, tilted his head slightly and concluded with, "Like I said, they can only make it for one week every month."

It wasn't long before Satterfield met a Geechy woman and ate the nautically forbidden red beans and rice. Three months passed before the Shore Patrol, the Navy's version of Military Police, caught him and dragged him back to the boat. When he was caught, he had been hiding under a Geechy woman's bed. Because the Navy did not know what they were dealing with, the punishment was very light.

Despite the shaky start to his naval career, in a few years Satterfield became a very disciplined sailor. Later, he transferred to another boat, the *USS Finback* and became their best diver. His primary assignment was a nuclear mechanic. But diving was his true love. For him, being a diver on a nuclear submarine was the most exciting job in the world. He never knew when his services would be needed, but when he got the call, it meant trouble. Though a diver was always on call, he couldn't idly sit around and wait to get that call for action. Divers were required to work another job and still be ready to don a wet suit at any time, even if it meant being awake for twenty-four or forty-eight hours straight. Satterfield knew being a diver was a hard-knock life. They received more tricks than treats from life. The weak of heart were not invited. The weak of heart could never make it on the *USS Finback*.

"Broady, pay attention!" Satterfield yelled out in the middle of his briefing. Although Broady looked as though he wasn't listening, he was. And Satterfield knew it. But he barked the reprimand for the benefit of anyone who wasn't listening.

Seaman Broady, all six foot four inches and 285 country pounds, looked up and responded, "Yes, sir!" Broady was fresh meat. Everybody called him "NUB," the submarine acronym that stands for non-useful body.

"Don't call me sir," Satterfield retorted. "My parents were married, and I work for a living," he added, snidely.

As soon as the statement had left Broady's mouth, he knew he had made a mistake. It had only been eighteen weeks since he had graduated boot camp, and six of those had been spent in diving school. But, he should have known better than to call his senior enlisted, "Sir."

Although Satterfield had ferociously jumped on Broady, he had actually taken a liking to him in the two weeks he had been on board. He liked the fact that Broady was a hard worker and by far the boat's best swimmer, both in speed and endurance. But, even though Broady was a hard worker, he had the talents and potential to become so much more. Satterfield recognized this and rode him hard, hoping it would help him to grow. Yet, how well Satterfield liked Broady was of no consequence, it was actually a rare occurrence for Satterfield to address Broady by his name.

The *Finback* surfaced about one hundred yards from the Norwegian vessel. The high winds tossed and rolled the submarine. Below deck, several sailors lost their sea legs, finding it difficult to walk without being tossed into steel piping and machinery. Many of the sailors moved around the boat with garbage bags tied to their belts. The garbage bags were used for catching vomit. Later, the sailors could compare and rate the contents of their garbage bags and award artistic awards for both color and texture.

Once the submarine surfaced, Satterfield and his team awaited the order to deploy. Although they had not been waiting long, their anxiety levels made it seem as if they had been waiting forever. The Navy was infamous for its *hurry-up-and-wait* syndrome.

Satterfield listened intently on the X160J Sound Powered-Phones. When he heard the order from the Engineering Officer of the Watch (EOOW) to open the Main Sea Water cross-connect valve and shut the port Main Sea Water suction valve, he knew it would not be long. This action was always done prior to divers entering the water. It prevented the large seawater suction valves, which were hidden below the water line on that side of the sub, from sucking a diver into it.

When he received a growl on the X160J phone thirty seconds later, he answered, "Machinery 1—Petty Officer Satterfield."

The canny voice on the other end replied, "Machinery 1—Con, you have permission to drain and open the upper hatch and commence the rescue operation. God be with you."

"Drain and open the upper hatch. Commence rescue operation. God be with us, aye," repeated Satterfield. The upper hatch was opened. Fresh air rushed up and out of the submarine. Once the hatch was completely opened and the pressure equalized, the direction of flow reversed, causing the outside environment to overcome the inside environment. Rain, cold wind, and near-freezing water invaded the submarine. The weather topside was much worse than Satterfield had expected. A deep-gray sky loomed above. The black water was choppy and flecked with white-foam. Stepping out onto the weather deck, wearing his insulated diving suit, it was all he could do to keep from being washed overboard. Holding fast to the cold, water-beaten upper hatch, he yelled an order down the hatch to the other divers to secure their lifelines as soon as they got topside.

Petty Officer Satterfield tried shielding the driving rain from his scrunched eyes with his hand. Still, the cold rain saturated his thick eyebrows and long eyelashes, while stinging his face. But, with great effort Satterfield could see the sinking ship off the starboard bow. He estimated the distance to the Norwegian vessel to be about the length of a football field.

Just prior to leaving port, permanent ladder rungs were welded to the side of the sail in preparation for decommissioning in the shipyard. This ladder made it possible for someone to climb from the submarine's topside deck up to the Bridge. Satterfield understood why the Commanding Officer had decided to load survivors through the Bridge Hatch and the Machinery 1 Hatch at the same time. It would reduce the amount of time the *Finback* was on the surface. Normally a submarine would stay submerged below a storm and ride it out upon a smooth laminar layer of water hundreds of feet beneath the surface. It was not designed to operate on the surface amidst hurricane level winds, at least not comfortably.

The winds were blowing the *Finback* toward the sinking vessel, which meant the return trip to the *Finback* with the lifeboats was going to be shorter. They would have to come back against the wind, however, and the *Finback* might have to turn the screw, the propeller, to avoid being driven into the sinking ship. Turning the large, powerful screw when divers were in the water was always a dangerous operation. It could suck divers into it at almost any speed.

"POW, POW, POW." The successive exploding sounds of three CO_2 canisters meant the tough neoprene lifeboats had inflated. Satterfield's team was trained well, performing every step of their procedures with precision. The entire team, except for 19-year-old Broady, had trained two years for an emergency like this. They were ready. But Broady, who had been on board the *Finback* for only a few weeks, was ready also and eagerly welcomed this opportunity to prove it.

All three lifeboats were tossed into the roaring North Sea. Then, Satterfield and two other divers plunged into watery tempest, also. The rough water made it difficult for the men to climb into the lifeboats. Although each man wore an insulated suit, the temperature was still low enough for him to feel the surge of cold. Each man shivered.

Once the divers had climbed into a lifeboat, the remaining three divers jumped into the water, each carrying a floatable box. Three two-man teams were formed, each working flawlessly, opening the crates and installing the small, powerful engines on the lifeboats. The cold divers, bobbing like frozen, red apples in a washing machine, then quickly climbed into their boats. Satterfield looked up and spotted Captain English on the Bridge of the *Finback*.

The captain had been on the Bridge since the *Finback* had surfaced. He had donned the army-green, foul-weather gear, but the force of the storm had rendered his gear impotent.

"He should be down below," Satterfield thought, noticing the captain's skin had turned a deep red, almost purple color, from exposure. But Satterfield knew there was no way the *Finback's* captain would consider going below during a dangerous rescue operation like this. Staring up at his tough captain on the Bridge, he marveled how his captain withstood the storm conditions while controlling his massive nuclear fighting boat.

With a hand salute to the captain, Satterfield deployed his team. Captain English returned the salute then yelled something to Satterfield. However, in his hurry to deploy, Satterfield missed the last words he might ever hear from his captain. The distance between the two and the raging storm made it almost impossible for Satterfield to hear and see the captain; the bridge was located 60 feet above the topside deck. The words spoken from the captain's freezing face were, "May God be with you." But Satterfield neither heard the words nor saw them form on the captain's frozen lips.

The storm gave no mercy to the *Finback* or the Norwegian fishing vessel. The three lifeboats fared much worse as they traveled toward the sinking vessel. With only two men per lifeboat, there was technically not enough weight in them. Once they were full of men, the lifeboats would perform much better on the rough seas.

Boat one, carrying Satterfield and another diver, and boat two, carrying Broady and another diver, arrived at their destination in just a few minutes. Satterfield had ordered boat three to stop and pick up survivors that were in the water. Even with the roar of the sea and wind, Satterfield's loud baritone voice could still be heard. "Start pulling survivors out of the water near the ship. We'll get the survivors off the deck until we are full. When you're done, assist us at the bow of the ship."

By the time the second lifeboat reached the nearly sunken vessel, Satterfield was preparing to shove off to deliver his living cargo to the *Finback*. "I'll send the number three boat to help you get the rest of the survivors off the ship," Satterfield yelled, his voice in fierce competition with the sounds of the raging storm and sea. At once, Broady climbed onto the deck of the ship and assisted most of the crew of the Norwegian vessel into lifeboat number two. Soon, the third lifeboat arrived.

Maneuvering was difficult but the third lifeboat managed to come alongside the bow of the ship about thirty feet forward of the number two boat. They began assisting the number two boat in the off-loading of the last survivors. As Broady began to help one of the last crewmen waiting to board the second lifeboat, he noticed embroidered "scrambled eggs" on his ball cap. "He must be the captain," Broady thought.

The captain of the fishing vessel was a middle-aged man with a square jaw and lines resembling dried, jagged river basins etched on his face and neck.

"Let me help you, Sir," Broady said, respectfully. He extended his large hand to escort the captain off the deck of his sinking ship. Instead of the grasping the seaman's hand in return, however, the captain eyed Broady with a puzzled look. It was as though he had never seen a Black man before. Then he noticed the arm patch on Broady's right arm. It was an American flag. The captain pushed Broady down onto the hard deck and ran toward a hatch, now at a 35-degree down angle, leading back into the ship and toward his stateroom. Slipping before reaching the hatch, the man fell hard onto weather-beaten, metal and wood hybrid deck. He quickly picked himself up and turned toward Broady, the blood on his face mingling with the rain that covered his purplish face. Beneath his thick eyebrows, his eyes appeared to shed tears of blood.

The captain yelled something in a language foreign to Broady that didn't sound positive, then disappeared inside the ship. Broady thought the language was Russian but he knew for sure it wasn't Norwegian. The only part he understood was "Yankees." Broady paused briefly. He looked at the number two lifeboat and then scanned the horizon.

Realizing Satterfield was probably back at the *Finback* by now, he glanced over at the number three boat and then back toward the number two boat. "Y'all go ahead back. I'll catch a ride with boat three," he yelled over the storm to the petty officer in charge of boat number two. With that, Broady dashed toward the same hatch the captain had entered. He slowed as he approached the hatch, not wishing to make the same painful mistake the captain had made.

Though Seaman Broady avoided making the mistake the captain made, he made a different one that was a thousand times more deadly. Unfamiliar with the ship's layout, Broady frantically searched for the Russian captain. There was not enough time to memorize his way out in case there was a need to exit in a hurry. He had prepared well for the mission with respect to his gear, but it was beyond him to think to bring breadcrumbs. With blind faith, he continued to search for the captain knowing with every second that passed, another portion of the vessel disappeared beneath the frigid, raging water line. Inevitably, the ship would sink. But this was not a linear relationship. Even though there was still plenty of ship left above the water line, there would come a time when the displacement of water afforded by the ship would be to too low and instantly sink.

At the end of a passageway, Broady opened a lightweight metal door with veneer paneling, and peered into what appeared to be the Captain's Stateroom. "I've heard of going down with the ship, but this is ridiculous," he said, pushing the door fully open.

Suddenly, Broady heard three loud sounds, and almost at the same time the top section of the door shattered. He hit the deck, immediately, avoiding the flying bullets "I'm here to help you, sir! I come in peace," yelled Broady, seeking cover behind an aluminum locker. He knew it wouldn't provide protection from a bullet, but at least it hid him from view.

"What have you to do with peace? You fall in behind me!" the captain responded, his English broken.

Broady sat frozen. He didn't have a gun. He looked down at the sheathed knife strapped to his leg. Removing the knife, he positioned it at the ready, knowing it would be useless against a semi-automatic weapon. His thoughts were interrupted by the sounds of a door flung open, violently, followed by running footsteps. He peeked around the locker and saw the captain had exited through an aft door and rushed down the passageway to what turned out to be the Wardroom.

Following at a safe distance, Broady descended the passageway, his teeth chattering. As he got closer to the doorway of the dimly lit wardroom, he saw the captain sitting on a bench, clutching the gun in his calloused hand while feverishly working on a missile mounted on a table.

Unable to simultaneously hold the gun and work on the missile, he looked around, sweat and blood leaping off his brow with each quick movement of his head. Broady, with a large lump in his throat, quickly ducked to avoid being seen. Once the captain was satisfied he was alone, he laid the gun beside him on the bench. Seeing this, Broady sighed.

Suddenly, the ship listed hard to the port side, causing the gun to slide off the bench and across the deck, stopping in the middle passageway that ran through the Wardroom. It wasn't far from the captain, but was at least twenty feet from Broady. Broady was now in the captain's line of vision. They eyed each other, apprehensively. Then the captain made his move. He dived for the gun. Broady ran toward the gun. When he saw the outstretched arm of the captain, Broady knew he couldn't reach the gun before him.

He threw the diver's knife at the captain's wrist, knowing once the knife hit its mark, it would buy enough time for him to get the gun. He watched it travel through the air, turning ending over end. Just then, the ship rolled even further to the port side, causing the gun to slide further away from the captain's outstretched hand. The captain had just landed on the deck and now he slid with the roll of the ship.

The blackened blade hit its mark. But it was not the intended mark. The serrated tip protruded through the other side of the captain's neck. The blood bubbles made a gurgling sound as they oozed from his wound. Then the captain died.

"FRACK!" Broady said, running toward the body. "Why did he have to go for the gun?" Broady asked aloud. He yanked the knife from captain's neck. The sound of a knife tearing through flesh was sickening. He then wiped the warm blood from his knife and returned the blackened blade to its sheath.

It was then that Broady's attention was drawn to the flashing Light Emitting Diode display (LED) on the missile. Because of the list of the ship, Broady had to climb uphill where it was mounted on the workstation.

"So this is what the captain was working on," said Broady. Examining the missile, he noticing the three-bladed yellow and magenta symbol on the casing. He couldn't read the Russian words but he recognized the universal yellow and magenta nuclear symbol. Chills ran down his spine. The LED display read thirty minutes, and was counting backwards.

A nuclear bomb would not only blow up the fishing vessel but a large section of the sea as well. If the *Finback* were anywhere close this would mean the end of her, as well. The *Finback* needed to submerge and get several miles away before the missile bomb detonated. Broady ran from the wardroom. He headed toward the hatch through which he had earlier entered the interior of the ship.

The hatch was the only thing standing between him and survival. Forcing open the rusty hatch, he met the raging storm again. Once on deck, Broady again struggled, climbing uphill toward the bow of the ship, desperately hoping to board the lifeboat. Suddenly, his heart plummeted. Visibility was bad, but he was able to see the last lifeboat on its way back to the *Finback*. This was the mistake he had made earlier; he had not asked boat three to wait for him. A very minor detail, indeed, but it had produced a major and potentially life-ending problem.

He checked to make sure his knife was secure in the sheath, activated his locator beacon, and dived into the frigid sea. Even with a full thermal suit, the freezing water almost took his breath away as he swam toward the *Finback*.

At first, he thought he was gaining on the lifeboat, a misconception caused by the onset of shock. His arms felt heavy and tired. Every stroke became a chore. The temperature of the water wreaked havoc with his breathing, making it hard to keep from inhaling the cold water.

Petty Officer Satterfield stood topside watching the number three lifeboat approach the *Finback*. He also scrutinized the survivors of the fishing vessel still being off-loaded and escorted below deck. He watched, with particular interest, the last survivor to come aboard. This man was dressed completely in black, from his watch cap and pea coat to his turtleneck shirt and dungarees. Unlike the other survivors, he did not appear to be in a rush to get below and out of the storm, but simply meandered around topside, occasionally, looking at the sinking vessel with interest.

Suddenly, the hairs on the back of Satterfield's neck stood up. "Where's Broady?" he asked, directing the question toward Smitty, the Petty Officer in charge of the number three lifeboat.

"He didn't come back with us. I thought he was in the number two boat," explained Smitty. "No one told me he was supposed to be riding back with us."

Simultaneously, Satterfield and Smitty looked at the sinking fishing vessel. "Oh, my God," Satterfield said, seeing the last section of the fishing vessel disappear into the North Sea.

"He's out there!" yelled the Lookout Watch on the Bridge, through a mouthful of freezing rain and brine. Looking through binocular lenses covered with beads of water, he stated again, "He's out there."

"Where?" someone topside asked. "Over there! Swimming this way!" the Lookout Watch responded, pointing in the general direction of where the fishing vessel had been.

Replacing the earlier sight of the vessel was a small slither of blinking hope, the locator beacon. Satterfield dove into the water and climbed into a lifeboat. He knew even though Broady was wearing a thermal suit, the water was extremely cold and it wouldn't be long before Broady slipped into hypothermia.

The open throttle of the little lifeboat caused the rain and wind striking Satterfield's face to feel more painful than before. He could see Broady in the distance still swimming toward him, but the almost horizontally-blowing, high-velocity wind made it harder and harder to see. Blinking for a second, he almost lost the spot where he last saw Broady. With the fishing boat sunk, there was nothing Satterfield could use as a reference point. Each time

Broady bobbed below the stormy water he remained submerged longer.

"Hang on, man! I'm coming," Satterfield yelled into the storm. He saw Broady sink once again, hoping it wasn't the last time.

Broady resurfaced, and to Satterfield's surprise, he was only ten yards from the lifeboat. Quickly throttling down, Satterfield pulled him into the boat.

Broady collapsed into the bottom of the lifeboat, shivering like a man operating a jackhammer in a fetal position. His speech was waterlogged; he was coughing up water. And he was freezing. "Da-da-dere's a nuuu-kear bum on the chip . . . ," he hammered out, making an attempt to point in the direction of the now sunken boat.

With only two people in the lifeboat and the throttle wide open, the little boat raced toward the *Finback*. Though short, it was a bumpy ride as the little lifeboat launched itself off the crest of each mighty wave only to crash back down to its trough on the tumultuous seas. Finally the bow of the neoprene lifeboat flattened momentarily as it collided with the HY-80 steel of the submarine.

"Get everyone below! There's a nuclear bomb on that ship and it's going to blow!" Satterfield yelled.

Urgency seized the ship but the crew of the *USS Finback* was trained well. By this time, most of the surviving crew from the fishing vessel had been escorted below deck; the only people left topside were some of the *Finback* crew, the captain and the Lookout Watch on the bridge. And then there was the mysterious man dressed in black Satterfield had noticed previously.

"We have to get out of here now. XO, secure the Machinery Room 1 Hatch and have the remaining survivors board through the Bridge Hatch," the captain ordered, grabbing the yoke of the sound-powered phone from the Lookout Watch and speaking directly into it. "Unfortunately, we don't know how many megatons that bomb is so we have to be miles away when it goes off!"

Some of the men started climbing to the Bridge in order to enter the submarine. "Move it, move it! Get your butts below," barked Captain English as each man entered the sub. He now rode his men hard to get them inside as quickly as possible.

He could read fear in some of their faces. But he didn't mind fear; it only indicated they were human. What the captain didn't want to see, especially at a time like this, was confusion. He knew his job was to prevent confusion. He marveled at how fluid his crew operated under this enormous anxiety. One by one, the crew entered the boat by way of the Bridge Hatch. Most of them were not using the steps on the ladder. They held on to the stainless steel cylindrical rails and slid down to the inner hatch. From there, they grabbed the next set of rails and slid into the Control Room.

Captain English looked at the face of every crewmember entering the boat through the Bridge Hatch. He made a mental note that these were some of the men who would receive citations later. That is, if they survived this ordeal. Then the captain looked back toward the Machinery 1 Hatch that had just been secured. He turned to the Lookout Watch and ordered, "Confirm that the Machinery Room-1 has been made 'ready for dive.'"

"Confirm Machinery Room-1 'ready for dive' aye," repeated the Lookout Watch. The captain would hear this order spoken five times before he would be satisfied the action was carried out properly. Once spoken by the captain, the Lookout Watch would repeat it back to the captain, and then the Lookout Watch would speak the order into the sound-powered phones. On the other end of the phone, a person would repeat the order to the Lookout Watch. Once that order was carried out, the person on the other end of the phones would report it to the Lookout Watch. The Lookout Watch would repeat it back to the person on the other end, and then repeat it to the captain. The Navy's efficient, practiced, and polished routine of repeat-backs and redundancies drastically cut back on mistakes due to miscommunication, especially on its nuclear submarines.

"Very well," said Captain English. He turned around in time to see the last man entering through the Bridge Hatch. This man had a black jacket and a black watch cap on. The captain quickly recognized him as one of the fisherman from the Norwegian boat.

"Tell Control to stand by at the bottom of the ladder and escort the survivor through Control," ordered the captain, turning in the direction of the Lookout Watch.

The Lookout Watch then repeated the order. Turning back, the captain expected to see the survivor descending down the ladder. Instead, the mysterious fisherman stood there, glaring at him, the wind and rain beating heavily against his face.

One hand held onto the sail's ladder rungs that led to the Bridge. In the other hand, he held a pin-less grenade. Instinctively, the Lookout Watch reached for his side arm but Captain English stopped him with a quick look and then turned to battle the fisherman in an eye-to-eye stare.

The man glanced down the ladder in the direction of the Control Room. He then returned the captain's stare. Now, the hard, sea-beaten, cold, face had a smirk chiseled on it. Before the fisherman could act, he felt a molar-loosening pressure exerted against his right jaw.

Captain English nearly lost his balance when he released the blinding left cross that even the Lookout Watch hadn't seen coming, even though his job was to lookout. The fisherman let out a groan, loosened his grip on the ladder rungs, and then landed on the metal surface of the starboard fairwater plane. As he fell backward, however, he launched the live grenade downward through the hatch.

The grenade fell toward the Control Room. Instinctively, the captain kicked at the grenade with the side of his foot. The fisherman laughed sinisterly as he spiraled downward, off the plane, into the cold, black sea.

Instead of landing in the Control Room, however, the grenade fell to the side of the escape trunk. "Tell them to dog the lower hatch!" the captain blasted. This time instead of repeating the order, the Lookout Watch yelled it directly into the phones.

"Dog the lower hatch, nooow-ugh!" His communication was suddenly interrupted. With his head slightly lowered, he hadn't seen the open-hand thrust to his chest delivered by the captain. Again, he failed to lookout. He fell overboard from the top of the Sail. Only his lifeline prevented him from falling to his death, or strangling from the phone line strapped around his neck.

Captain English jumped off the other side. He heard the metal clanging of the hatch being shut just as his nylon safety harness reached its end, abruptly stopping his fall. Next he felt the cold steel and the hard-textured paint used to coat a submarine as his face scraped alongside it like a pendulum. Because he knew their lifelines were more than strong enough to support their weight, Captain English had no fears for himself or the Lookout Watch. He knew, too, if the steel casing of the submarine could withstand water pressure at crush depth, 1,800 feet, then it surely would protect them from a grenade blast. Suddenly an explosion emanated from the top of the open access panel of the Bridge. His blood pressure rose, his head felt as if it were being crushed between two boulders, and his ears rang violently. The dark gray background of the horizon lit up with a vivid video display as fire shot out of the top of the Bridge, looking and feeling like exhaust from a jet engine.

Despite the damage and possible loss of lives, it was beautiful. The amber blast took on a strobe light effect giving the appearance of glowing yellow raindrops suspended in midair. It looked like the sky was raining golden pieces of jewelry with internal lights. As the hot, glowing fragments performed, the wind assisted their parabolic dances across the dark canvassed sky. Then the amber lights disappeared, some quickly, some slowly.

The blast had caused an External Hydraulics oil line to rupture spewing flames from the Bridge access panel.

In the Control Room, pandemonium ensued. Red and yellow alarm lights flashed at various non-synchronous frequencies. Horns and alarms sounded off like a New York City traffic jam, as young sailors frantically tried to silence each alarm and make reports to the Officer of the Deck.

The OOD interrupted the reports when he ordered the lower hatch to the Bridge opened. "Check the drain valve open, then open the hatch," he said. The Auxiliaryman of the Watch climbed the ladder and tried to open the heavy metal hatch, which had been slightly damaged from the grenade blast. It offered some resistance. When he finally forced it open, an inferno of a high-pressure hydraulic fire forced him from the top of ladder. He fell a good seven feet onto the deck below, backside first, the extreme heat vaporizing the sweat from his face.

"Fire in the Bridge access trunk!" yelled the OOD over the 1MC. "Secure External Hydraulic pump number one. Damage control party lay to Control." Casualty drills are not uncommon aboard submarines. But when the rest of the crew heard the report, they could tell this was no drill.

When the OOD finished the casualty announcement, he received an incoming report. Straining to decipher the report amid the high background noise transmitted through the phones, he was finally able to ascertain that it was the captain.

"The captain's alive," he announced to everyone in the Control Room. A loud cheer rang out.

"Secure that noise!" the OOD rebuked, trying to listen to the last part of the captain's message. The entire control room fell into a dead silence, as the other sailors also strained to hear the captain's message.

"Ahead flank, heading 270, get us the heck out of here. Remember we still have a bomb below us, gentlemen," the captain added calmly. The speaker crackled one last time, and then went dead as if there were only a void on the other side.

The Throttleman in the Maneuvering Room, the control room for the engineering spaces, heard the rings of the bell and saw the indicator move violently from "All Stop" to "Ahead Flank." Immediately, the 7MC, the communication link between Control and Maneuvering, bellowed the order from the OOD, "Cavitate! Cavitate!" The Throttleman quickly adjusted his indicator to match the one from Control so they would both indicate "Ahead Flank." He then looked toward the Reactor Operator and waited for him to shift main cooling pumps to fast speed, pull control rods and increase nuclear reactor power as the Engineering Officer of the Watch (EOOW) monitored. That didn't take long.

Maneuvering and the rest of the engineering spaces were isolated from the forward part of the ship by the reactor tunnel so they did not know the severity of the situation unfolding in Control and Topside. However, they knew if a submarine were sitting on the surface and there was a sudden bell change from "All Stop" to "Ahead Flank," the fastest speed, danger was imminent.

The Throttleman opened the throttle and rapidly brought the main engines up to flank speed. The engine room, which had projected a low hypnotic hum only a few seconds ago, was now alive and loud. They shifted all Main Sea Water pumps and Auxiliary Fresh Water pumps to fast speed and the twin steam turbines quickly built up speed. Now the engineering section anxiously awaited any clue as to what was happening Topside.

The explosion had ripped and badly burned the section of Captain English's nylon lifeline that rubbed on the edge of the bridge. Nonetheless, his face badly scraped and bruised, he had managed to pull himself to the top of the Bridge despite the wind and heavy rain. He climbed to the top of the Sail, and then lowered himself down on the other side to attend to the motionless body of the Lookout Watch, who also had been dangling by his nylon lifeline. The captain could not stay on top; the heat from the fire was too intense.

He immediately checked for a pulse, eyeing the shrapnel imbedded in the Lookout's temple. There was none. Without hesitation, the captain untwisted the phones from around the Lookout Watch's neck but didn't remove them. The yoke assembly was severely charred and brittle, crumpling in his hand. Speaking directly into the mouthpiece, he calmly, but firmly gave an order to the Control Room, wondering if it would reach Control. Moments later, Captain English received the answer as the stern part of the boat came alive. The screw began cavitating, churning up black water with white foam, then the boat picked up speed.

Looking off the starboard side of the boat, the captain spotted the mysterious man who had tossed the grenade and jumped overboard. His body bobbing, he had succumbed to the water's frigid temperature. His face had turned blue. The only indication Captain English had that the man was still alive was an occasional batting of the eyelids when the cold water washed over his face. "He'll be a frozen shark snack in a few minutes," the captain said. "I wonder if Control got *all* of my message." Again, he received an answer in action.

The *Finback*'s rudder moved and turned the boat to starboard, right into the direction of the man in the water. The steel hull made contact with him about midship. Captain English saw him disappear below the surface, then reappear further aft alongside the boat, briefly. He submerged again. "God, have mercy on him," the captained remarked. The next time the captain saw any evidence of the man in the water was a few seconds later. The once black foamy water emanating from the screw was now a purple color with crimson colored foam.

A deep orange color illuminated the horizon. At some distance it may have looked like a sunset. But it was now moving across the open sea. Black smoke and orange flames billowed from the top of the Bridge as if it was a smokestack. The bend in the flames became more apparent as the *Finback* approached top speed.

The heat, acrid smoke, stinging rain and the winds made the task of holding on to the top of Bridge increasingly difficult for Captain English. He still dared not trust his lifeline, not now, after it went through an explosion. His hands were in rebellion. The back of them felt the impact of stinging, high velocity rain and cold wind. But his palms and fingers felt the extreme heat from the hydraulic oil fire. Even in the arctic air, steamy beads of sweat formed upon the captain's forehead. He managed to hold on for over five minutes while the fire burned violently within the sail, and the *Finback* desperately raced away.

"Captain, are you all right?" inquired a young A-Ganger, Auxiliaryman, his smoke-smudged face peering from the top of the sail. Carefully and skillfully, he had ascended the ladder to the Bridge, while carrying a PKP fire extinguisher in one hand. The A-Ganger had successfully extinguished the fire. The captain, worrying about the time of detonation for the nuclear bomb had been completely caught off guard by the young sailor.

"Tell the XO to make preparations to dive!" the captain yelled to the young sailor.

"Sir, the grenade damaged the upper and lower hatch. The upper hatch will not shut at all and the lower hatch will shut but won't dog. Sir, we can't dive," explained the A-Ganger.

Locking the captain arm-in-arm, the A-Ganger reached over the side of the Bridge to help him up. Suddenly, a thunderous noise sounded in the distance. Both men stopped moving. This sound commanded their full attention. They looked at the horizon aft of the ship. *"Get below and shut that hatch!"* the captain yelled.

"But, Sir, what about you?" asked the young sailor, already knowing the answer. "I won't leave you."

The sea started at a low rumble and the *Finback* echoed. Dishes, tools, and analog gauge faces shook violently. The XO sounded the collision alarm and the klaxon blared.

Then it showed itself over the horizon, a monstrous wall of dark water, at least three hundred feet tall. It was easily the answer to a suicidal surfer's dream. The towering structure was magnificent and powerful.

"*Get below now!!*" the captain yelled once again. "That's an order. Shut the hatch and save the boat. I'll be all right. I've got my lifeline." This time, the orders from the captain, plus the sight of the enormous watery wall were enough to make the young sailor follow orders, instantly. He quickly tossed the fire extinguisher overboard and slid down the ladder into Control, reaching the bottom of the ladder as Captain English pulled himself to the top of the Sail.

The rainstorm now seemed insignificant compared with the looming danger. Captain English, exhausted, cold and wet, struggled to determine how close the liquid grim reaper was. The watery wall completely covered the horizon as it approached the *Finback*, making it tough for the captain to accurately judge how close it was to his boat. Unconcerned about the metal objects his head would strike, he immediately dived for the Bridge access opening to get out of the direct path of this liquid wall.

He never made it into the Bridge, but instead he was momentarily suspended in mid-air, as the force from his dive very briefly equaled the force from the rush of water. His attempt to dive for safety was very quickly negated.

Meanwhile, the A-Ganger stopped his descent down the lower ladder so he could shut the hatch. But before he could reach up to shut the lower hatch, he was met with a large water hammer.

Tons of water pounded against the *Finback*'s hull. Control was drenched as one long continuous slug of water roared down the escape trunk. The young A-Ganger slammed headfirst into the stainless steel grate mounted at the bottom of the ladder.

Red and yellow, steady and blinking, visual and audible alarms went off simultaneously at almost every station in Control. But no one cared about the alarms now. Stopping the water from coming in and saving the boat was the immediate goal of the struggling sailors. Upon initial impact, the boat had violently listed to starboard. Everything that wasn't secured, such as tools and seasick sailors became missile objects. The lighted panels in the Control Room dimmed like flickering candles, then lost total illumination. As water spewed throughout the circuits, most short-circuited and blew fuses, but some were still alive with energy, arcing, sparking, and sizzling.

After the nuclear tidal wave passed, the seas calmed, and the storm subsided. It was as though the destructive force of the nuclear blast had won a battle with Mother Nature and somehow blown the fierce storm away.

The *USS Finback* was now dead in the water. The nuclear reactor scrammed when the ship had listed badly. Frantically, in the aft end of the boat the EOOW started the emergency procedure for bringing the reactor critical once again and restoring propulsion. The crew in the forward section of the boat worked on ground isolation and pumped the water out of the boat.

Meanwhile, the executive officer climbed the ladder to the Bridge. Reaching the top, he anxiously looked about for the captain. His heart dropped down to his knees when he saw the Lookout Watch, dripping with seawater, hanging lifelessly by his nylon line over the side of the Bridge. He then saw Captain English's lifeline. He pulled it up. But, found no one attached to the end. The lifeline had been severed and only frays of material were left where the captain had been attached.

Once propulsion was restored to the *Finback*, they searched for the captain for several hours while repairing the hatches. Without any other options remaining, the XO reported to the crew and Submarine Atlantic Forces in Norfolk, Virginia that Captain English had been lost at sea.

Crippled, but now seaworthy after repairs were made to the escape hatch, the American submarine slowly submerged and disappeared under the now calm, but even colder sea. At 1000 feet below the darkness and murkiness of the North Sea, Satterfield and other sailors exchanged silent glances. They acknowledged each other's silent words and pain with a nod. Satterfield thought to himself, "Yes, we did lose a good friend." The news report faded out.

*****

Julian carefully avoided making eye contact with his wife, Jasmine, who had entered the recreation room while he was watching the news report about the *Finback*. She was in the mood to make love. It had been almost three months since the last time they were intimate and Jasmine was desperate. Now, she sat beside him, rubbing his chest. For the last few months Julian had thwarted all her advances.

When he finally turned to Jasmine, he thwarted her again by telling her Bill would be picking him up for work in a few minutes.

Bill Rousseau was Julian's best and only friend. They were also work associates. The mention of Bill's name caused Jasmine to instantly stop what she was doing and stand up. She became silent, folded her arms across her chest and stared disdainfully at her husband. Her mouth was barely open as her bottom lip quivered with anger. If she had lasers in her eyes she would have instantly disintegrated Julian. It wasn't the mere mention of Bill's name that incensed her. After all, she and Bill were actually good friends. It was that Julian had dared to mention Bill's name while she tried to be intimate with her husband. She had thought Julian, and Bill, who was unmarried, had spent an abnormal amount of time together over the last year.

However, he and Bill was spending that extraordinary amount of time working on a revolutionary invention at La Del Technologies in Troy, Michigan, an upscale suburb of Detroit. They had been working on it for years but now they were at a critical stage of its creation. Though they had been working on it for almost four years, Jasmine knew nothing about it.

It was an invention so revolutionary it would change the way every human thought of time and space. And, so secret only half a dozen people in the entire United States knew about it. This Time Warp Machine would actually warp a section of time, making it nonlinear, within a certain projected area. In theory, this would allow a person within this confined area the ability to move backward or forward in time. Dr. Julian Barnes and Dr. William Rousseau had completed the machine almost eighteen months ago but up until now it had never been tested on humans. They had first tested it on inanimate objects, then organic matter such as fruit, and then on animals. That night, the test would be the first test on a human. Julian knew it would be either he or Bill who would go through the time warp first. The other would stay behind and monitor the equipment. He then realized if it were he, and something went wrong, then that evening would be the last time he would see Jasmine.

Julian now returned Jasmine's stare. His eyes held the promise of passion. Leaning forward, he kissed her lightly upon her lips. Just then, the doorbell chimed and a computer announced Bill's arrival at the door. As usual, he had arrived precisely on time.

"Hello," Bill called out, upon entering. There was no mistaking his combined French and English accented voice. Julian quickly rose from his seat, as if ashamed to be caught in a position that looked like he and his wife were being intimate. Turning to walk out the door, he bade good-bye to Jasmine. Just before he reached the door he turned back and looked at his wife. He walked back to her, pulled her into his arms, kissing her long and passionately.

"I love you, Babe," Julian whispered. Exiting the room, he walked backwards and watched her like a man who had just fallen in love. When he was gone, Jasmine stood silent and motionless. Passion showed on her face. But was chased away by anger and then desire. She slowly exhaled, looking totally confused.

CHAPTER 2

"Computer, increase illumination." At this command the room lighting instantly brightened, relieving Ham from straining his eyes as he studied the blueprints for the La Del Technology building.

At that moment the computer announced, "Ricochet is entering your home."

Ham looked up from the long, light blue tinted, glass table where he had been studying the blueprints and said, "You're late! What the heck kind of time are you on? — C.P. time? You were supposed to have been here twenty minutes ago so we could go over these blueprints!"

Normally, Ricochet was very punctual, usually showing up for appointments twenty minutes early. Ham knew if he was late it had to be for a good reason. He just wanted to get his verbal jabs in early.

C.P. time is a euphemism used when referring to a person who is notoriously twenty minutes, or more, late for most engagements. It is most used within the African-American culture. Which is apropos since C.P. originally stood for Colored People. It started during the era of slavery in America. Those slaves too afraid to runaway to the North stayed behind on the plantations and conducted their own form of rebellion and sabotage. They slowed the work process, which sometimes resulted in a beating, by arriving late when they were sent on errands or assigned tasks. But, when slavery ended C.P. time did not end, entirely. And now it transcends all ethics groups and religions. Some even use C.P. time to describe those people who notoriously arrive late for church. Only in that case, C. P. stands for Church People.

Entering the room, Ricochet looked at Ham with his usual confident sneer and replied, "I was with your mama. The only reason I'm here this early is because she told me she had to get her beauty rest. Most women can get by with a few catnaps. But, we won't be seeing your mama any time soon 'cause she needs a coma.".

Ham and Ricochet had been best friends since meeting at Drew Junior High School in Detroit. Ironically, they had become best friends after someone wrongfully started a rumor, saying, they were talking about each other's mother. They were the smartest students in Mr. Rakecki's wood shop class so someone started the rumor to turn them against each other. Ham and Ricochet fought. Afterwards, realizing they had been set up, they became extremely close.

They remained best friends throughout high school at Cass Tech, Detroit's academically elite high school. Since the beginning of their friendship, Ham and Ricochet had engaged in the verbal bantering known as 'playing the dozens.' Therefore, as usual, Ham responded quickly, "You're just mad because when you were born, your parents almost lost you. Your mom using the bathroom and your father was in there shaving. When your mom was ready to flush, your dad just happened to look over and stop her. He told her. "Wait a minute . . . don't flush! It has eyes!"

Ricochet started to chuckle. Then he burst into wild laughter, as he saw Ham do his best to imitate an armless piece of human waste floating in water, blinking its eyes helplessly, like a newborn baby trying to focus when it comes to life.

After the laughter subsided, Ricochet responded, remorsefully. "Man, I'm sorry for talking about your mother. I really shouldn't have said anything about her. She's always helped me out. When I was hungry, she brought me food. And when I was stuck in the snow, she rescued me and brought me something to drink."

He then walked over to Ham, put his arm around him, looked him straight in the eyes, and said, "Your mama is a real saint. A real Saint Bernard!"

They both laughed. But Ricochet wasn't through just yet. "And so sweet! Your mom's so sweet she's got a tattoo of Aunt Jemima on her leg. Or is that her picture? Nice hat. But seriously, your mom is sweet. She's so sweet that compared to her, cotton candy tastes like salt pork!"

Ham knew he had been set up, and set up well. His only redemption was to do his impersonation of a laughing Ricky Ricardo. Ricochet hated it when Ham laughed at him like that. It made him feel insecure about his jokes.

This levity could have, would have, and many times did go on all night. But, as far as Ham was concerned, this night was not going to be one of those nights.

"Look!" Ham said, slightly irritated, "Since you were on *Colored People Time*, I started on something else."

"Oh, am I bothering you now?" Ricochet asked, not concerned at all.

At this point Ham could end the verbal volley either by being quiet or by stumping Ricochet with a riposte he wouldn't be able to respond to. Like seeing a comet, stumping Ricochet and shutting him up, were rare occasions. Ham chose the latter, recklessly.

Answering Ricochet's question with a question, Ham queried, "Do bears go to the bathroom in the woods?"

Ricochet responded, immediately and effortlessly, "No, not *Polar* bears." He grinned with victory.

But Ham didn't know when to lick his wounds and go home. He tried again. "Do pigs fly?" he asked, believing there was no smart answer for this.

Again Ricochet responded, immediately and effortlessly, "Well, I didn't think so until I found out your girlfriend had to pay extra for her airline ticket. She was passenger fifty-seven, fifty-eight, and fifty-nine at the same time."

Ham threw his hands in the air and turned away saying, "Why don't you go into the den? Please, give me about thirty minutes."

He didn't wait for a reply. He simply started studying the blueprints he had been looking at prior to Ricochet's arrival.

Although Ham could hold his own against his best friend, he decided to ignore Ricochet until he got serious. Once Ricochet realized there would be no more witty repartee from Ham he would lose interest. True to form, Ricochet shrugged and went into the other room to watch television.

Ham and Ricochet were electronic corporate thieves, ECTs, electronic mercenaries who broke into corporate computer systems and stole secret designs and formulas. They usually worked for corporations wishing to get a competitive edge by stealing information from other corporations. Sometimes, the U.S. government contracted for their services, for what it called, "foreign relations".

In the old days, computer hackers had been able to use regular telephone or cable lines to obtain such information. Due to the high number of corporations being put out of business because of information theft, Congress had ordered the creation of an electronic network for transferring information across America. Any time information was sent over the network it received the electronic equivalent of a police escort. Therefore, it became easier to break into a corporation's premises and steal secrets than to attempt to do it over the communication lines.

That evening, they were after the plans for a new handgun bullet expected to be twice as effective as existing bullets but 95 percent less likely to kill a person. They contained subminiature electrical generators, which converted the high kinetic energy developed from the bullet's velocity into electrical energy. These new bullets supposedly did not penetrate the skin, but instead flattened like miniature ultra-thin pancakes upon impact. Once they impacted the skin, tiny electrical conduits would deliver an electrical shock that would render a person unconscious for thirty minutes. They were in the initial stage of development at La Del

Technologies' facility in Detroit. Although the U.S. government had not sponsored this project, they would award a multi-billion dollar contract to the first company that developed these bullets.

Ham and Ricochet had been hired to break into and steal the secret for the bullets from La Del Technologies. They were the best ECTs money could buy: Ham as a break-in artist and Ricochet as a computer code hacker. Together, they were a highly sought after and a highly paid team. But, for the two best friends, when it came to working together, irritation was normal. When they were just hanging out or having fun, there wasn't a problem. Only when they worked together would a problem manifest itself. Maybe that would explain the Tums Ham chewed constantly when they worked together. Because of Ricochet's nonchalant, happy-go-lucky and comical attitude Ham would easily become very irritated with him. Ham always believed things of a serious nature required serious thinking, not jokes. Deep down, Ham never realized he was jealous of his best friend, who was his complete opposite.

Ricochet sat in the den watching television. He had reclined into the teal leather recliner in what looked like a comfortable position. Yet, Ricochet always found it difficult to relax in his best friend's house. The house was well-decorated, very contemporary, and boasted of the latest in design and equipment.

For example, the recliner Ricochet sat in was not an ordinary leather chair. It was actually a command post from which one could control most electronic or mechanical functions throughout the entire house, from watering the grass to toasting bread. All controls were integrated into the arms of the chair. What Ricochet didn't like about the room and the entire house was it was too neat. In Ham's house everything had its proper place—that is, except when Ricochet purposely left things where they didn't belong just to see his friend's reaction. When it came to his friend's home, Ricochet believed Ham suffered from a slight case of 'Ungaritis,' being too neat, like Felix Ungar, and it was his job to help him.

The television Ricochet watched was a singular self-contained unit mounted on the far wall. It was no thicker than a modern picture frame, and its plasma screen was ten feet by eight feet in dimension. He sat, watching ESPN 8. There was a story about Barry Sanders coming out of retirement and breaking Emmitt Smith's all-time rushing yards record in the same year the Detroit Lions won the Super Bowl, January 2006.

Ricochet was an avid Detroit Lions fan. So much so, when he went to the games he would shave his head bald and paint an exact replica of the Detroit Lions helmet on it. He suffered throughout the bad years when the Lions never made it to the Super Bowl. But he stayed their most loyal fan, sometimes driving twelve hours in snowstorms, on Thanksgiving eve, to make it to the next day's game. He knew exactly what was wrong with the Lions and was never too shy to tell anyone.

But everything changed when the Lions hired Matt Millen as Chief Executive Officer. He negotiated with Barry Sanders, the star running back, bringing him out of retirement. Ricochet thought one of Millen's smartest moves was giving the Lions a tougher image. A darker, fiercer-looking blue replaced the sissy Honolulu blue uniform. And a fiercer looking lion replaced the Wizard of Oz-like, namby-pamby, cuddly lion painted on the helmets.

Ricochet had called the organization and asked them to change to a fiercer looking lion that would instill fear in their opponents, a lion with fire coming out of his mouth and behind.

They asked him, "Why would you have fire coming out of its behind?"

Ricochet replied, "If you saw a lion with fire coming out of its rear end, wouldn't you be scared?" They chose to pass on the rear end suggestion but implemented most of the other ideas. With these changes, plus obtaining a top-rate quarterback, the Lions were able to win the Super Bowl in five years. The Lion's story ended and a commercial followed.

"Computer, scan," Ricochet ordered. He had forgotten he was originally recording the special about Barry Sanders on compact videodisc.

The computer answered back, "Scanning programs." The channels scanned up, pausing just briefly enough so one could determine whether or not he wanted to watch that station. On CNN there was a report about Al Gore running for President of the United States. This time his strategy would be different from the failed 2000 campaign. He had selected Hillary Rodham Clinton as his running mate and allowed Bill Clinton to manage his campaign for him.

The channel changed again and this time Ricochet saw a news report about an American submarine attempting the rescue of a Norwegian fishing boat. The reporter announced eleven people were lost at sea and presumed dead during the rescue attempt, including the captain of the submarine.

Ricochet joked, "Well, I guess the crabs are going to have 'human-cake' sandwiches tonight." "Computer, TV off," he ordered. Leaving the room, he went to help Ham as he playfully imitated the claws of a crab pulling flesh off of a human carcass.

*****

It had been decided by a flip of a coin Bill would be the first human to attempt time travel. Julian was disappointed, but he knew the decision had been fair. Nevertheless, Julian understood his part of the experiment would be just as important as Bill's. The time travel machine was designed so one person could travel through time and back without another person being left at the base station. Since this was the first documented attempt at time travel, however, it made sense that all precautions should be taken to prevent anything from going wrong.

It was 11:30 p.m. Julian and Bill completed their pre-flight checklist. They had agreed to call this a pre-flight checklist since they would actually be flying though time. Just then, Julian remembered he had told Jasmine he would be home around 9 o'clock. He was now more than two hours late. If he kept ignoring her, he knew his wife would eventually do one of two things: leave him or kill him. Still, he and Bill had been working on the Time Machine for years, and that night was the night they had worked for, for so long. Nothing was going to stand in the way of it now, not even his marriage.

The actual time travel machine was a self-contained unit that stood no higher than four feet. It was spherically shaped and its surface was that of a symmetrical multi-faceted diamond. Though its nuclear fusion power supply was self-contained, there was a solar panel mounted on each facet, which gave it a backup power supply. The time ball sat in the middle of a platform that determined the boundaries of the Time Machine; anything on that platform would be projected in time. After the time ball reached its destination and it was time for it to return, the time ball would project its own boundaries. This caused a heavy strain on the power unit and the solar cells. But if the weight of whatever was being transported in time were not too great, the time ball would handle it.

Weight was of great importance to the operation of the Time Machine. The weight of the object or objects being transported would always have to be entered into the computations during the pre-flight checklist. This was a critical step. If someone entered the wrong weight, it could drastically change where and when a person would end up in history or the future.

The control station, standing approximately thirty feet from the platform, monitored everything about the Time Machine that could be monitored, including the body temperature and heart rate of the traveler. Though the control station had adequate shielding, its distance from the platform was far enough so any stray transmissions from the time ball would not interfere with any of the readings in the booth.

With all pre-checks complete, and both Bill and Julian ready, the experiment started. Bill stepped onto the platform and Julian entered the control room. Julian set the destined time for ten days in the past and the auto-timer for fifteen minutes. The experiment would commence in fifteen minutes unless he aborted it from the control room. Besides having a visual display of the remaining time, the computer also made an audio announcement every two minutes, the last minute and a countdown from twenty seconds. Looking through a window in the control room, Julian gave Bill the thumbs up. He also made a mental note that Bill had donned his chromafilter glasses.

The first time Julian and Bill had sent a live animal through the time warp it returned unconscious. They learned that during time travel, the spectrum and intensity of light the time traveler was subjected to overloaded the optic nerve of most animals. So, Bill had designed the filter glasses to prevent it.

The glasses were impregnated with a lead and titanium alloy but they looked normal and cool enough to wear on the streets. Although they were called chromafilter glasses, they did only minor filtering. Designed to work like a prism, the glasses actually separated each color from the white light thus preventing it from being too intense. Julian didn't bother to don the pair he had in his lab jacket pocket since he wasn't traveling that evening.

"Eleven minutes. Dr. Barnes you have a telephone call on line one," the female voice of the computer announced. Julian swore under his breath. Bill teased him. They knew it had to be Jasmine. His wife was bothering him at a critical point in the experiment, but Julian wasn't mad because of that. It was more because he had still forgotten to call and cancel their late dinner date. He would get home real late, if he ever got home at all that night.

Julian knew his marriage was in serious trouble. And now, things seemed to be coming to a head. It was pretty ironic that Julian and Bill were working on an invention that would allow humans to travel back and forth in time but his marriage was about to disintegrate because of lack of time spent with his wife.

Checking his watch, Julian picked up the telephone in the control room. He knew he could only talk to Jasmine for five minutes. If he were going to apologize and sweet-talk his wife, he had to be quick. He had always been a smooth talker, but somehow he didn't think he was going to talk his way out of this one. The dinner date for this evening had been requested by Jasmine two days ago so they could talk out their marital problems. But, because he was not going to show up, he knew Jasmine would think he didn't care about her or their marriage. The truth was, he did care but he had his priorities wrong. He put his work before his wife.

Expelling his breath heavily, Julian collapsed into one of the chairs. He propped his feet up on the control panel and gazed at the far wall in the control room as if it were a window. He couldn't see through it, although if he could, he might see more than the blackness of the night, which had given itself up as a backdrop for the brilliant stars. If only he could see through the wall, then perhaps he could see what was already taking place under the cover of night, on the grounds just below his fictitious window. "Baby, I'm sorry . . . ," he started.

*****

Hidden in the night's background outside of the electric fence that surrounded the La Del Tech building, Ham and Ricochet, dressed in black assault gear, waited patiently. As usual, Ham had taken every precaution to make sure his plan to break into a building was flawless. There wasn't a place in existence he couldn't break into--so he thought. Most men have fantasies of women or untold riches. Ham's ultimate fantasy was to break into Fort Knox, not for the gold – just so he could say, he did it. That night, they weren't looking for gold, but something worth as much as gold to a certain corporation.

Apparently, through normal leaks, a rival corporation had learned the new bullet technology was at the La Del building. They had decided to acquire the information from the Troy building because it was a far less secure facility than the Detroit site. The Detroit facility was located inside the First Union/Wachovia Bank Northern Headquarters Building, one of the most secure buildings in the Midwest.

It had only been thirty minutes since Ham and Ricochet had taken up a position in the twilighted black foliage. Yet, to Ricochet it seemed like at least three hours had passed. He watched the effect of the thin crisp air being expelled from Ham's mouth while Ham peered through the night-vision binoculars. Ham was counting the security guards and timing their movements to make sure everything matched his previous scouting expeditions.

"Something's wrong," he said, his voice low and unsure. Ricochet was hungry, bored and cold, and really didn't want to hear anything was going wrong. He wanted to either get on with the job or go home.

"You're darn skippy something is wrong! I'm here freezin' my butt off, lying here on the cold ground, when I should be at home with your mama, who, by the way, is a member of the Mo-Tee-Sah Tribe."

"Not now, Rik. This is serious," Ham replied. He had previously scouted this place and noted the number of guards, while timing their routines. But now, everything was completely different: too many guards and a totally different schedule for the patrols. Either something else was going on inside the La Del

Building, or they were expected. Either reason would cause the increase in security and the irregular security schedules.

Ham asked, "What do you think?" He was still slightly mad at Ricochet. He was not so mad, however, he discarded Ricochet's input. Ricochet could crack almost any computer code, which meant he was a very logical person. But he was also very intuitive.

When Ham asked him what he thought about continuing with the mission, it took Ricochet about ten seconds to answer. If it took him that long to make a decision it usually meant he was considering intuition along with his logic. Working off pure logic, it normally took him at the most two seconds. Ricochet finally answered; his decision could have been influenced by the fact that he was cold and hungry. It could have also been influenced by pride, because they had a reputation of being successful every time they took a job. But when Ricochet finally answered, he looked Ham straight in the eyes with a degree of seriousness Ham rarely saw from him. "I don't know why, but I've got this feeling that we need to be inside that building, now," Ricochet answered.

The bushes rustled ever so slightly in the crisp night air as Ham and Ricochet emerged. They approached the electric fence. Ricochet was a lot more apprehensive about approaching it than Ham. He paid close attention, trying to avoid the surging grid. He was now sure the buzzing sound he heard was not bugs in the night but electrical pulses from a giant bug zapper that now stood less than eight feet away from him. Ham, however, brushed right by Ricochet and walked directly up to the fence. He didn't say anything, but his body language did.

"What are you stopping here for? Get out of my way, you 'fraidy-cat." These would have been the words spoken from Ham's body and from his haughty eyes. At that point Ricochet was following Ham's lead. It wouldn't be his show until they got inside to the computer.

Approaching the electric fence, Ham's head bobbed up and down, and from side to side, surveying it for a few seconds. If he had any fear of it, he surely didn't display it. Going back to the bush he had been hiding behind, Ham pulled out a black camouflaged duffel bag. From within it, he removed a black leather tool bag, a cylindrical object, thick black rubber gloves, a thick black rubber mat and a transparent safety facemask.

"Is that what I think it is?" Ricochet whispered, an undertone of concern apparent in his voice. Ham didn't answer him verbally. He just nodded and went back to what he was doing. Ricochet always felt uneasy around liquid nitrogen. It wasn't fear, just uneasiness. This time Ham approached the fence with a different purpose in mind. Just a few minutes earlier, he had surveyed the electric fence. However, this time he was looking for points he had previously marked in his mind. It wasn't long before he found them, again.

He had already donned the rubber gloves and laid the rubber mat in front of the fence. Pulling the transparent face shield over his face, Ham stepped onto the rubber mat with the cylinder of compressed liquid nitrogen in hand. He began to spray out a square section of fence. Ricochet felt a cold shiver surge down his spine; he took a step back.

Cautiously, Ham measured out a section just large enough for two men to simultaneously pass through, despite the overhead-connecting pipe. This would be left in place to provide rigid support and conductivity for the fence.

Instantly, the fence became more alive and began glowing a bright-orange color, and then changed quickly to a lifeless dark color.

Both men held their breath, their hearts racing as they wondered if anyone else had seen the glowing light. Ham carefully removed a rubber mallet from his duffel bag and started tapping the treated section of fence. Immediately it crumbled into metal flakes. Upon hitting the ground, the flakes twinkled into fine metal dust, which made a metallic sound like a wind chime in a cool, balmy breeze.

Again, they went motionless. No guards had been aroused by their efforts. Only the sound of a howling dog could be heard coming from a far off hillside. Spreading the rubber mat on the ground through the square opening in the fence, Ham reminded Ricochet the pipe was still alive with electricity. It had to stay there so as to complete the electrical circuit, and not activate a perimeter alarm.

Now, it was time for Ricochet to go into his duffel bag. He removed two black shock resistant cases. They contained what looked like two elaborate video cameras with spiked tripods. One unit was marked 'RECORD,' the other 'TRANSMIT.' Ricochet hurriedly walked along the fence about twenty feet from the manufactured hole in the fence, still aware of his distance from the fence. He spiked a tripod there, into the ground, and installed a camera.

Ham spiked the other tripod in front of the section of fence they had just disintegrated and installed the other unit. After a few minor adjustments, a green 'SYSTEMS OK' light came on. Tripping over the duffel bag when he stood up, Ham fell face forward toward the live electric fence. He couldn't stop his fall, but was able to gather his thoughts in that instance. And what he thought was that he was about to die, not like a man, but like a piece of burnt toast.

When his face was an inch from the live grid, Ham felt a choking pressure at his throat. "Is this what death feels like," he wondered. Then he realized Ricochet had caught him by the back of his jacket collar.

"Saved your life! You owe me," Ricochet said, smiling. Ham sat on the cold ground for five seconds, attempting to compose himself.

They were now ready to enter though the fence, carrying their duffel bags and all the equipment, except for the camera equipment. It was Ham's philosophy that the more they carried with them, the less they would have to pick up on the way out, especially in case they had to make a speedy exit. When they got to the other side of the fence, Ricochet reached into his pocket to retrieve the remote control device. He found it, but he also found something else. It was a compact videodisc of the Barry Sanders show he had recorded earlier that night. He was at a loss as to how it got into his pocket. He tossed it back into his duffel bag without any further concern, and then used the remote control to activate the two camera units he had just installed.

The first unit was indeed a camera but also a transmitter. It was set up to take a video picture of a large section of fence and transmit it to the other unit, which projected the signals as a holographic image. In this way, the system was set up to fool more than the most casual observer that the fenced perimeter had not been compromised. And it looked very convincing. The only way someone would be able to detect it was if they had ventured too close to the fence. As highly charged and lethal as the fence was, no one would want to get that close to it, purposely.

Once inside the La Del Technologies building, Ham noticed certain corridors that normally had its sensors and cameras on were mysteriously unprotected. Also, low security areas were now elevated to higher security levels. Now, Ham was worried. If it weren't for the fact that the physical layout of the building matched the layout that had been supplied by the company that hired them, exactly, he would have sworn they were in a different building. He reached into his pocket and pulled out a roll of Tums. This time it wasn't Ricochet's fault.

Ricochet, a couple of steps ahead of Ham, had only studied the layout for this building and the route of entry Ham had devised, once. Yet, he would have been able to find his way around in the

La Del Tech building blind if need be. This worked out well because Ham was pre-occupied as they made their way through the C-wing into the A-wing.

"Stop!" Even though it was spoken in a low raspy voice, the layer of quiet in the corridor was enough to make the voice reverberate. Instantly recognizing his friend's voice, Ricochet stopped. Without looking at Ricochet, Ham said, with a puzzled look on his face, "The motion detectors in this corridor should not be active. They are. We'll have to circumvent them." This was the part Ham liked the best about his profession. Whenever someone invented something that had to do with security, he wanted to be the first one to come up with a way to counteract it.

The infrared motion detectors worked by sensing the change in heat as a person walked across the invisible infrared legs emitted from the motion detectors. So far, the best way known to defeat the motion detectors was to navigate past them at a pace of five inches per minute. However, Ham had stayed up late the previous night, not only studying the layout of the building, but also coming up with a more efficient way to circumvent the system.

If the infrared sensors detected the heat changes as a warm body moved across the room, what would happen if the body moving across the room were not warm at all? Ham's first plan was to don asbestos insulating suits, spraying the outside of the suits with a carbon dioxide fire extinguisher before going through the detected area. However, he decided that solution would require them to carry too much bulky equipment, and was too noisy. To do so, would drastically decrease their ability to get in and back out in a hurry. And its probable success rate was too low.

He came up with another method. It was so simple he wondered why no one had thought of it before. Perhaps his idea was like Ricochet, so simple it was complicated.

Ham reasoned, if a body needed to be cold in order to move through an area undetected, then why not just heat up that area.

That way, relatively speaking, the body would be cold in respect to the ambient temperature. It was, after all, the law of physics.

Reaching into his duffel bag, Ham pulled out a device half the size of a shoebox. While setting it up, he stole a quick glance at Ricochet. Being one-up on his friend was a feeling Ham thoroughly enjoyed. He then explained this new toy was actually a very powerful laser generator he had modified twice. At first, he had equipped it with a beam intensifier, which made it possible to cut off a Master Lock at two hundred yards. The second modification, which Ham had made the night before, was to install a molecular kinetic diffuser. This took the concentrated beam of light and spread it out. Now instead of a small intense laser beam, the Portable Laser Unit (PLU) would have the effect of a headlamp with a range of about thirty feet. Actually, it would act more like a very powerful heat lamp with the ability to heat an area in excess of one hundred and fifty degrees.

Ham continued to work while he explained this to Ricochet. Taking a telescopic rod, he ever so slowly pushed two LED thermometers into the corridor. Beads of sweat began to form on his brow. If he inserted the thermometers too fast he would instantly trigger the motion detectors. Although one thermometer would have sufficed, Ham believed in redundancy. Having a back up system was something he did not take lightly.

The thermometers, strategically inserted, monitored the temperature of the corridor. Ham watched each one with a concerned eye. At 103 degrees they would be able to proceed through the infrared-monitored area, so he set the thermometers to beep at that temperature. But, at 120 degrees, the automatic sprinkler system would be triggered, instantly alerting security and the fire department.

The plan was to energize the PLU and proceed through the zone at a speed somewhat slower than a slow walk, and then turn the PLU off at the other end by remote control. Ham lifted the aluminum cover and pushed the manual switch mounted on the PLU. With the PLU energized, the corridor took on an eerie red color, much like the color of blood.

Despite his cool demeanor, it was very apparent that Ricochet was not quite comfortable with the horror movie-like effect. To Ham, Ricochet was the most fearless person he knew, but he had one weakness. He was scared of horror movies and any of their special effects. He dreaded looking at pictures of Frankenstein, not to mention listening to just a few notes of eerie scene-building music from a horror movie. So, when the red glow of the PLU illuminated the corridor, Ham had to chuckle to himself a little. Almost as soon as the PLU came on, Ricochet's eyelids looked as though they opened another five centimeters. Ham was reminded of a similar incident that happened in a haunted house about ten years ago. He thought about it as he sat, waiting for the temperature to reach 103 degrees.

*****

It was a balmy October 30th some ten years earlier. In Detroit, this night was called Devil's night. It was a night that not only the Detroit Fire Department, but also most of the city feared. In the 1960s and 70s, it was merely a semi-harmless night in which mischievous youths ran amuck around the city, throwing eggs at houses and cars, overturning trash cans and dumping the contents onto the streets, writing words on car windows with soap bars, and dousing stray cats with lighter fluid then setting them on fire.

But, as society changed, it had escalated from the harmless pranks, except for the cat thing, to serious crimes. Arson became the number one crime committed on Devil's Night until Detroit's newly elected 31-year-old mayor, Kwame Kilpatrick, ordered that all the abandoned buildings, a major target for arsonists, be torn down. He played a large part in revitalizing and bringing major corporations back to the city. Organizing citizen's groups to help patrol the city on Halloween eve, the mayor renamed it Angel's Night.

But that particular evening Ricochet and Ham had been drinking and were two sheets to the wind. Ham suggested they go to a haunted house. Agreeing to something like that was normally not what Ricochet would readily do. But, at that time he had an artificial courage brought on by Captain Morgan, the brand of rum he drank, that whispered into his ear, "You can do it!"

So off to the haunted house they went. Before entering, Ricochet got another idea from the captain. Getting into a huddle like two kids playing sandlot football, Ham and Ricochet conspired. "They got real people in there, right?" Ricochet rhetorically asked, his speech slurred. "Well, let's go in there, and when they jump out to scare us, let's jump them and kick their butts."

They had been inside the haunted house for two or three minutes. Doors squeaked of hinges begging for oil. Flashing strobe lights that must have been bought at a disco-tech "going out of business" sale fluttered and oscillated. Several staged displays of Frankenstein and Dracula unsettled Ricochet as they progressed through the haunted house's maze. The second-rate horror staging appeared out of almost total darkness. For the labyrinth's only clue as to which direction they should follow was the florescent markings on the floor, which were illuminated by the lowly lit ultra-violet black-light bulbs.

When Ricochet first entered the house he had been laughing, but as they progressed through the maze his laughter subsided to a faint echo, then a serious silence.

Taking the point position, Ham led the way through the dark passage. He turned to check on Ricochet. Then, he saw it. It froze even him in his tracks. Ricochet, not noticing Ham stopped, walked right into him.

Spinning around, Ricochet saw it too: a very tall white woman. Not a White woman, but a white woman. Painted very pale, she had a tear of dried blood that traversed her cheek between her right eye and her chin. Her jet-black hair, with a streak of gray, was almost waist length and she wore a long, flowing, black dress, which seemed to be controlled by wind currents. But there was no wind or draft. Because of her long hair and dress flowing back it looked as through she was teleporting through the air as she approached them.

Suddenly, from within the folds of her dress, she produced a butcher knife so large it could easily been mistaken for a pointed meat clever. Lifting the knife high above her head, her destination determined, she moved towards Ricochet to thrust it down into him.

Ricochet drew back his right arm and cocked it to throw a punch upwards toward the underside of her jaw. Though, he would have to jump to reach it. They were locked in this visual duel, the tall woman and Ricochet, only for a fraction of second. The woman, hired only as an actor to scare people, burst into loud laughter. Then Ham, looking at Ricochet, immediately broke into a laugh so hard he almost hyperventilated.

Had Ricochet had a hand held mirror, and had he been looking at himself he would have laughed immediately also. For in the terror of the moment the diameters of his eyeballs had increased drastically. In fact, his eyes were so big they could have caused stretch marks on his forehead. As it was, it took about five seconds, but Ricochet joined in the laughter. Needless to say, there was no beating up anyone that night, only on Ricochet's ego.

*****

They watched the thermometer in the corridor go from 77 degrees to 95 in less than a minute. Then as it read close to 100 degrees the temperature began to increase at a decreasing rate. Ham whispered, "Oh, I almost forgot." Opening a compartment on the PLU, he pulled out a remote control, aiming it at the PLU to test its remote feature. This step was going to be very important to them on the way out; they had to do everything in reverse. The check was satisfactory as the remote turned the PLU off and then back on.

The temperature reached 103 degrees and the thermometers emitted a low beep. Ricochet and Ham started down the corridor with the duffel bags slung over each of their shoulders. The corridor was only about 50 feet in length. Yet, because of the pace they had to walk to prevent triggering the alarm system, it seemed more like the length of a football field to Ricochet.

As they started down the corridor the temperature was a stifling 105 degrees and still rising. Ham had been monitoring the rate of increase of the temperature and felt comfortable they had plenty of time to make it to the end of the corridor then shut off the PLU before the automatic sprinkler activated at 120 degrees.

The corridor had an evil-red glow to it. In a matter of minutes the temperature reached 110 degrees. The humidity felt equally as high. Sweating profusely, Ham was amused when he looked back at Ricochet. He thought, "Man, his eyes are as big as silver dollars." After what seemed like an hour to Ricochet, they finally reached the end of the corridor. Brushing by Ham, Ricochet collapsed into a sitting position against the far wall at a tee in the corridor. Ignoring him, Ham reached into his pocket, and spun around to face the PLU and de-energize it. The thermometers were then reading 116 degrees.

He reached into his pocket for the remote control. It wasn't there! In a controlled panic, he immediately checked the rest of his pockets, almost punching holes in each pocket as he searched deeply. Ham's anxiety level, once very low, was now increasing at an increasing rate with each check of every pocket that did not produce the remote control.

Frantically, Ham looked back down the corridor and spotted the remote control on the floor, right beside the PLU. His heart dropped. He then looked at the thermometers; the temperature read 117 degrees. Someone was going to have to go back down the corridor and retrieve the remote and then come back through the red zone and cut off the PLU before the temperature rose to 120 degrees. He knew there was no way in the world he was going to convince Ricochet to go back down that red corridor, certainly not before the temperature rose high enough to trigger the alarm. So, without wasting any more precious time, he started back down the corridor, hoping he could make it back in time.

His pace was quicker than the last time, but he still had to respect the motion detectors. True, although the corridor was much hotter than when they had first come through, there was still a possibility the motion detector would detect his movements. The temperature was 118 degrees when Ham finally reached the remote control. His clothes were drenched with sweat. Bending over to pick up the remote control, large sweat beads from his forehead puddled upon the floor. Outwardly, he cursed at the remote control, as if it were to blame for being left behind.

The thermometers were still reading 118 degrees as Ham quickly made double-time to the end of the red zone as with silent, but energetic body language.

Ricochet encouraged Ham to hasten his pace. He had not seen a guard in what seemed like an eternity, but he still knew they were not alone in the building.

Once out of the red zone, Ham immediately let out a big sigh. The sprinkler system had not been activated. The thermometers were reading only 119 degrees. And, he had the remote control in hand. Surely, Ham had every right to celebrate. So far it had been an exciting but good day. All he had to do now was to push the button on the remote to turn off the PLU. He aimed the remote control down the silent red corridor toward the PLU, pressing the power button.

Nothing happened! He pressed again, and again, watching the remote control to make sure he was pressing the correct button. Still, nothing happened. He banged on the remote control desperately with his open hand, as if it were an old flashlight. Running out of options, Ham checked the batteries. Upon removing the battery compartment cover, his heart didn't just fall to the ground; it plummeted.

The brand name on the batteries read "SuperVolt." SuperVolt was the brand of batteries that were compared to Energizer batteries in the old Energizer battery TV commercials. SuperVolt batteries were notorious for running out of power at the most inopportune times. Now, the electronic chickens had come home to roost.

In disgust, Ham clinched his fists, still holding the remote control; he raised them toward the heavens and growled. Grasping the remote control with both hands, Ham snapped it into two pieces as easily as if it were a small, dry twig.

Simultaneously, the thermometers clicked to read 120 degrees, the sprinkler systems activated, pouring pressurized rain, and a very loud pulsating fire alarm blared in their ears. It was as if God were punishing Ham for blaming Him. The truth was Ham was just too cheap to buy Energizer batteries.

The water from the fire suppressing system struck the circuitry and the red-hot lenses of the PLU. The equipment burst into flames and the glass lenses shattered, violently, sounding a small explosion.

Grabbing his duffel bag, Ricochet ran down another corridor. Ham tried to stop him. He wasn't sure if that were the escape route he would recommend. But, it was too late. So, snatching up his duffel bag also, Ham sped off after his friend.

*****

It looked as though it was going to be just another quiet night at the security control station for Ruben Marberry. For that reason, he had brought his small five-inch color television. He was an avid Pittsburgh Steelers fan and he didn't intend to miss the game that night, just because he had been called in on his day off. The second half was just starting; Pittsburgh was losing to Detroit 17 to 3. Ruben sat up more rigidly in his chair, glancing over to his partner just as Detroit lined up for the second half kick-off.

Terry, the other security guard, was occupied watching the security monitors. That's when it happened.

It was as if a limit switch was installed inside the football. As soon as the football was kicked off of its tee to start the second half, the security station alarmed with life.

Ruben fell out of his chair with the sound of the fire alarm going off in his ears. Terry, who had been monitoring the control panel closely, turned to Ruben, saying, "We've got a fire on level 3-section B. The fire department has been notified."

Ruben and Terry could not leave the security station during an emergency, unless their safety dictated it. Serving as a damage-control station, their function was to coordinate emergency efforts. Ten seconds into the fire casualty, a second alarm on Terry's panel sounded. Again, very calmly, Terry informed Ruben of the condition. "We've got unauthorized movement on level 3-section D. The police have been notified."

*****

Ricochet had never been in the La Del Tech Building, yet, he was running through and negotiating the maze-like corridor at a frantic pace. Though he had looked at the building plans only once, and Ham had studied them for days, Ricochet knew this building like the back of his hand.

Ricochet was frantic, yet still in a focused mode. It was a chore for Ham to keep up with his partner; the added weight from the duffel bag he carried plus the extra weight of his clothes, which were still soaking wet from the sprinklers, made the run almost unbearable. But every time Ricochet came to an intersection in the corridor, he would wait until Ham caught sight of him before going on. Ham thought he had memorized the layout for the building, but due to the speed at which they were moving, he was now completely lost. In order for him to determine exactly where they were he would have to stop and collect his bearings. But there was no time for that, so he put his faith in his friend.

Ham was aware that without using the PLU unit, they were setting off motion detectors at every turn. He also knew if they were indeed setting off detectors left and right, then they were probably being tracked like laboratory mice in a maze, as they attempted to flee the scene. But he could not be concerned about that now; he realized it was more important to get out of the building. Ricochet slowed down as they approached the end of a corridor, pointing to a doorway marked "Stairs." He turned, saying to Ham, "That's our ticket." Neither man noticed another door to their immediate right with a lighted sign above reading, "TESTING IN PROGRESS. DO NOT ENTER."

Paying little attention to the fact he had tripped the door sensor, Ricochet opened the door to a stairwell that was isolated from the rest of the building by a heavy fire door. It was cold and quiet, with a heavy aluminized scent emanating from the material the stairs were made of. Upon entering the stairwell, Ham and Ricochet heard the distinct sound of a two-way radio.

"They're in the east stairwell-third level," Ruben blared through a bassless two-way radio, which a guard at the bottom of the stairwell carried. Though Ricochet and Ham were on the third level, the stairwell was so quiet they could hear the radio from the first level.

"We're on it," responded a voice with much more bass.

Now, Ham and Ricochet would have to backtrack to find an alternate escape route. However, before they could take a half step in the other direction, they heard what definitely sounded like people in a connecting corridor coming in their direction. They were trapped. With one security force closing up from the stairwell and another coming from the other end of the corridor, there were few or no options.

A confrontation imminent, the two friends stood back-to-back, weapons drawn. Suddenly, noticing something peculiar on the wall on his left, Ham lowered his weapon. Ricochet glanced at him quickly, then in the same fashion turned back toward the stairwell door so he would be ready when the guards entered. "What are you doing, man? We're going to be up to our elbows in alligators with guns and badges in about twenty seconds," he said, sweat now pouring from his brow.

Ham didn't hear his partner; he was busy scrutinizing the bulkhead. He ran a finger along the wall on what looked like a shape of a perimeter he recognized. He then reached into his pocket and took out what looked like a credit card.

"Now is not the time to order stuff from www.beneaththeunderdog.com. If you're going to do something brilliant, I suggest you do it quick!" Ricochet pleaded.

He didn't exactly know what was going on but he trusted his friend; Ham was not one to lay his gun down in a situation like that. Despite the subdued lighting in the passageway, Ham still found a soft seam along the perimeter. He activated a flush switch on the card, lighting a red LED display on the card. He then slid the card into the seam about one third of the way with the LED display still showing.

Ricochet could not tell how close the guards on the stairwell were, but he could feel them. He could hear the sounds of the security force rapidly approaching from the other end of the corridor, and he knew they were too close.

"Come on, man! You get us out of this and I promise to never talk about your mama again," he whispered? "I'll just use sign language," he thought.

As Ham slid his card around the seamed track, Ricochet noticed the LED display changing from red to green at different points. He deduced this was good by the look of satisfaction on his partner's face. Also, the shape of the seam Ham was outlining had taken the shape of something near and dear to Ricochet's heart, now more than ever. Ham traced the seam to the end, the LED display turned green and blinked and beeped three times. "Bingo!" the proud locksmith announced.

He had just found and picked the electronic locking mechanism of a secret access panel. Immediately there was a welcoming whoosh as the panel opened, equalizing pressure and revealing a room on the other side. Ham grabbed his duffel bag and entered. Not having to be told to follow, Ricochet immediately slipped through the panel, also.

This room was not on the plans Ham and Ricochet had studied just one evening before. But knowing where it led was not an immediate concern for either of them. To them this room was a sanctuary no matter how temporary it may have been.

As Ricochet closed the panel, the stairwell door burst open revealing a rather large, horizontally lunging security guard with his sidearm drawn.

Simultaneously, at the other end of the corridor another security guard, just as hastily, entered with his weapon drawn. "HALT!" they yelled. The deep bass voice of one of the guards resonated from one end of the corridor and the tenor voice of another projected from the other end. The two security guards were in sight of each other but they were also in each other's direct line of fire.

What sounded like a double clasp of thunder was actually two shots fired, almost simultaneously. Firing their weapons, both guards hit the deck. Neither guard moved a hair or a muscle in the dead silence that followed.

"Clem, Matt, don't try to catch them, we know where they are," commanded a voice from the two radios that had been dropped by the guards onto the hard deck.

"Do not attempt to engage the perpetrators. The police are on their way up," blared the radios. "I repeat, do not attempt to engage! The police are in the building and on their way up." Still, there was no response; only a cold, dead silence permeated the air.

Finally, a heavy voice softly called out, "Clem?"

"Yeah?" the simple reply coming from the other end of the corridor.

"You fool!" yelled back the first voice. "You almost shot my head off," looking at the bullet hole that had been drilled into the steel fire door just a few seconds earlier.

The dumbfounded security guard at the other end of the corridor simply looked up, saying, "Uh, sorry."

Detectives Clifford Brett and Rusty Vorhees were getting off shift. Rusty was giving Cliff a ride home. As the report came over the police radio about the intruders in the La Del Tech building, Rusty and Cliff were driving by the building. Cliff picked up the microphone and reported they would be responding to the call. Rusty did a 180-degree "Bat" turn, and sped directly to the front gate. The gate guards quickly let them through and directed them to the correct building.

Reaching the control center in the main building, Rusty and Cliff found the building guards monitoring the unfolding situation with the intruders on their panels. The guards briefed them quickly and told them the best route to the room Ham and Ricochet had mysteriously disappeared into, only minutes earlier. The two detectives checked their guns and proceeded to the third level.

*****

"Three minutes and counting," the computer-generated voice announced.

Julian heard that in one ear, and in the other ear he heard, "You don't love me anymore." The computer voice was a lot more pleasant. With the experiment still counting down, he had been on the phone entirely too long with his wife. Although his marriage needed a lot of shoring up, this was not the time to talk about it.

He and Bill Rousseau were on the brink of making history, the first documented successful time travel by humans, and it was all going to happen in less than three minutes. Still trying to get off the telephone with Jasmine, he heard another voice in his free ear.

This voice was Bill Rousseau's. "Julian, we've got a problem. I need you out here now!"

Julian knew if the slightest thing went wrong it could very well be a matter of safety. "Baby, we've got a real problem down here. I've got to go. Love you, I'll call you later." Those were the last words Jasmine heard. It was either fortunate, or perhaps unfortunate, for Julian that he did not hear the response from his outraged wife.

Julian spun his chair around quickly. A flashing red light on the instrument panel indicated there was a fire somewhere in the building. But there was no audible alarm associated with it. Looking up toward the monitors, Julian saw the switch for the alarm was in the silent mode. But, as he looked through the control room window, he would have been less surprised if he had seen whales riding bicycles. It was Bill on the time travel platform being held at gunpoint by two assailants.

"Get out here now, Dr. Funkenstein!" Ham ordered, brandishing his weapon toward the control room.

"Two minutes and counting," announced the female computer voice. Reluctantly, Julian left the control room, dismissing a quick thought to terminate the experiment. However, once the time travel sequence initiated, a force field would envelope the time warp perimeter, preventing anything or anyone from entering into the warp field, a safety feature added by Dr. Rousseau.

Julian now reasoned if it would keep things out, then it would more than probably keep things in. If only he could lure the two assailants into the field. They could trap them there, terminate the time travel, and hold them until the police arrived.

"I said, 'Get out here now!'" Ham once again barked. "And keep your hands up! Don't touch nothing."

Julian, with his hands on top of his head, walked out of the control room toward Ham, Ricochet and the besieged Dr. Rousseau.

"Get over there!" Ham snarled, grabbing the back of Julian's neck and pushing him onto the time travel platform. "And next time, don't take so long!" Julian's face hardened. But there was little that could be done while they had guns trained at their heads.

"One minute and counting," the computer continued, startling Ham and Ricochet.

Ricochet's voice quivered slightly as he asked, "One minute for what?" Julian only glared at his armed inquisitor. So, Bill explained what was going on, begging them to let him terminate the experiment.

Meanwhile, Julian thought, when Bill goes into the control room to turn the equipment off, he could stay on the platform until just before the force field is activated, trapping the two assailants inside. Ham and Ricochet wouldn't be able to shoot at them because of the force field. Still, Julian was going to have to let Bill know to not turn the Time Machine off until the last second, and then to leave the force field on.

"Bull! Ain't no such thing," Ham said. "What do we look like, a couple of Sam Sausage-Heads? Humph! You ain't said nothing." He added, slightly chuckling. "I'll tell you what! Ain't nobody doing any time traveling or any type of traveling until we get out of here. So which way out, mad scientists?"

"Twenty seconds and counting," the computer, like a nagging wife, reemphasized. By then, Julian decided he was going to have to turn the Time Machine off or it wasn't going to happen, because the force field would be automatically activated in ten seconds.

Julian turned toward the control room. "I must shut down this experiment," he pleaded.

Ham, snorting angrily, grabbed him by the back of the collar on his lab coat. "You want to be a mad scientist? Then I'll give you something to be mad about!" He struck Julian in the back of the head with the butt of his gun. Seeing it coming at the last moment, Julian tried to move out of the way. He only partly succeeded as it was reduced to a glancing blow. Still, it was enough to stun him. Blood spilling from his head, Julian collapsed upon the floor of the time panel.

"Fifteen, fourteen . . . ," the computer continued. Bill, who had been restrained by Ricochet until now, broke free of the chokehold. He rushed to Julian, offering assistance.

"Thirteen, twelve . . . ."

Then without warning, Ham and Ricochet were suddenly thrust into each other as two large cops simultaneously lunged at them from opposite directions.

Rusty and Cliff had planned to not fire their weapons upon the two intruders, given the close proximity of the hostages and the assailants. They also didn't want to make a bad hostage situation worse by trying to talk the assailants into giving up, since one, or both could panic and end up shooting a hostage.

Despite the ambush, Ricochet and Ham fought well.

" . . . Ten," announced the computer. Suddenly and without warning, a pellucid casing surrounded the perimeter of the entire time travel platform. It was the force field Julian had earlier considered; it was almost invisible except for a slight reddish tint. Although this made Ricochet slightly uneasy, it was not as deep red as the PLU lights. He stopped fighting for an instant, observing the field. During the struggle, Cliff had dropped his nightstick. It rested half on the platform and half off. When the force field activated, it cut the nightstick into two pieces, making a loud crackling sound and launching splinters airborne. Ricochet only glanced at the stick and force field, but it was long enough to give Cliff a costly advantage over him in their fight.

Ricochet felt intense pain in his back as Cliff drove him into the force field. Screaming in agony, he felt as though there were a thousand knives impinged in his back, all being twisted at the same time. This gave the effect of lightning as the force field arced and sparked on contact.

" . . . Seven, six . . . ," .The computer did not listen. It did not see. It could only do what it had been programmed to do. So it continued to count, much like a child playing Hide and Seek, with his eyes and ears shut, oblivious to what is going on around him as he counts.

Julian, who had been stunned by the blow to the head, began to recover. And, much like a stunned heavyweight fighter down on the canvas, responding to the referee barking out the count, "EIGHT!" Julian stumbled, falling back onto the platform. His vision began to clear; he knew instantly what was going on, where he was, and what was about to happen, not just to him, but to all six people trapped inside of this red glass-like chamber.

" . . . Three, two . . . ," continued the computer. Hearing this, Julian reached into his lab coat, pulling out a pair of the same type chromafilter glasses Bill had donned earlier. Hurriedly, he put them on. Turning, he was relieved to see Bill had his glasses on. Two cops he had not seen before and the intruders were fighting. He could not tell to whom the advantage was going; he was just glad he was not in the middle of it any more. "One. Time warp procedure has been initiated. Have a nice flight," the computer requested.

Even with the chromafilter glasses on, the light was intense. Julian couldn't see Bill or the others trapped inside when the Time Machine activated. Yet, he could sense they were still there with him. He saw an abundance of white light, but most of it was separated into different colors. This made any image appear to be washed out with rainbow shadows. He could see images and events of people that were very dynamic, as if he were right there as things were taking place.

Besides the euphoric sensation of floating backward through time, he was amazed at the array of colors surrounding him. It was as if all the stars in the universe were there, presenting a prismatic display of colors from their trailing tails. He saw all the colors in the visible band, yellow, blue, magenta, cyan, and many more. But, he was also able to see some colors in the infrared and ultraviolet range. He could make out faces and places as the colorful display of stars presented a pleasurable backdrop to the images: events and people from his past and from others' past. Normally, Julian was not a very sensitive man but he silently wept as he saw the actual destruction caused by wars, the expression on people's faces while they were being murdered, and mothers dying during childbirth.

Julian marveled, too, as he saw parades for heroes, fathers and sons playing catch, and lovers embracing so tightly that only their closeness concealed them.

Suddenly, with absolutely no warning, the images ceased. There was a low sounding thud, along with the painful feeling of a large solid object hitting his head; he had fallen off the platform onto the ground headfirst. Dirt and rivers of mud were present where previously there had been tears on Julian's face.

He could now verify what he had already known. Six people, not just one, had traveled back in time together. He saw Bill standing on the platform observing the surroundings. And he also saw four unconscious figures. He recognized them as the two intruders and the two police officers who had interrupted the experiment and involuntarily become a part of history.

Chapter 3

A landscape of rolling green grass, the scent of lilac and many other spring flowers, and what appeared to be an abandoned farm set the welcoming stage for the group's arrival to an unknown place and time in the past. The acres of land looked as if they hadn't been worked in at least a year. To their left, the clearing ended and the woods started. To their right, stood a barn and some abandoned farmhouses.

"Where are we?" Bill asked.

"I have no idea where we are or what year this is," Julian replied, rubbing blood off the back of is head. "But I do know we have about ten minutes before these guys wake up. Let's split up and try to find some answers. You check out that building," he said, pointing to the nearest farmhouse. "I'll collect all the weapons and watch them." Meet me back here in five minutes."

The rickety porch of a house was littered with balls of dead brush that had been deposited there by the wind. Bill peered through the dirt-covered windowpane of a door that screamed for a coat of fresh paint. There were no locks on the door. Looking around to make sure no one saw him, he entered the house.

Several pictures hung crookedly on the walls. A rickety table, couch, bed, three dust-covered chairs, and a couple of kerosene lamps were the only other articles in the house. Bill wiped away the dust from one of the pictures and saw what he assumed to be the happy family that once lived there.

Picking up a brown, fragile newspaper from under the table, he blew away the dust. Bill sneezed. The headline read, "Chief Justice Taney Rules – Negro Scott Still a Slave." He folded the paper, put it in his lab pocket, and headed toward the barn. From the house it was only a short walk. What was odd to Bill was there was only one door for the house, just the front door and no back windows.

What a deathtrap this would become if ever there were a fire, he thought. The barn was in the back of the house, which meant a person would have to go out of the front door and completely around the house to go into the barn. It probably never occurred to them to install a back door.

The wide, weathered, wooden barn door revealed the history of its maintenance schedule very well. It creaked loudly as Bill opened it. Finding nothing of importance, he started to leave, then noticed two old, rusty machetes hanging on the wall to the left of the door. The handles were made of two pieces of wood that sandwiched the butt of each blade. Two leather thongs secured them. Hanging beside the machete was a fairly long rope. He hastily relieved the wall of all of these items and ran back across the field, toward Julian.

Meanwhile, Julian collected all the guns from the unconscious cops and robbers. He put all the firearms, except for two, which he kept out for him and Bill, into one of the duffel bags that had been carried by the robbers. Meeting up with Julian again, Bill showed him the newspaper. The masthead read "The Richmond Times." And the date was March 6, 1857. Raising an eyebrow, Julian was overwhelmed by the sudden severity of the turn of recent events. He sat back on the time platform, lines appearing on his forehead, trying to figure out exactly what had gone wrong.

"The Time Machine was only set to go back ten days in the past. The added weight from the extra five people must have thrown off the settings," he deduced. However, before Julian got a chance to become comfortable in the thinker position, Bill informed him of the reason he brought back the rope and machetes. "Good thinking," Julian commended, as he and Bill began tying up the four unconscious people.

"I bet they're going to be as mad as hornets when they wake up," Bill said, smiling quirkily. It probably wasn't going to be the most popular decision in a few minutes, but it was probably the safest for *all* parties concerned.

There was no guarantee when the foursome recovered they were not going to try to kill each other. This way, Julian thought, he and Bill could take as much time as needed to explain the gravity of the situation to them. What the scientists needed to impress upon them was they were all in this together, and most importantly, the Time Machine had not been designed to make a return trip with a significantly different total mass than what it left with, yet. In other words, the same weight that was sent had to be returned.

Ten minutes later all of the bound men woke. They were still slightly groggy, but they were coherent, just mean as hornets and snakes. Rusty, Cliff, Ricochet, and Ham discovered they had a common bond, besides the ropes, they were prisoners.

Now that they had their undivided attention, Julian and Bill explained to them, the Time Machine, where they were, why they were unconscious and how the mass had to be the same to return. Once they were satisfied their prisoners weren't going to kill each other, they released their bonds.

There was still heavy tension and animosity in the air once they were let loose, as the two opposing sides automatically paired off. But Julian and Bill had guns in their hands, and would use them if necessary.

All day—if one could say "day," since they just traveled backwards in time over one hundred and fifty years—it seemed that luck had not been on their side. Dusk was rapidly approaching as the red setting sun fell over the faces of all six travelers. Suddenly, there was a scream in the distance coming from the woods. All heads turned in that direction.

Without a discussion, all of them went to investigate the source of the scream. "Let's go!" said Julian, brandishing his weapon. Rusty and Cliff looked at the bag containing their weapons; they were not used to knowingly entering into life threatening situations without their guns at their sides.

Upon entering the woods, everyone was walking in front of Julian. So without anyone realizing it, Julian stashed the bag of firearms behind a tree. They made their way through fifty yards of thicket, slowing down only to cross a small creek.

Rusty's police training had taken over and he had assumed the point position. Getting closer, they were able to hear other voices. Approaching a glade, Rusty could see the people who went along with these voices. He motioned for the others to come closer, quietly. What they saw boiled the anger within them.

"Hey Jack, she's a pur-ty one, ain't she? I can undastan' why she might wanna run away the firs' time, but I dunno why she would run away from some hansum devals like us?" The other eleven White men laughed in response to this. They surrounded Kat, an attractive slave. Her dress had been torn half off, and her face was bloody. Even with the abuse to her face, her beauty was unmistakable. The men, who so savagely harassed her, had tracked and hunted her down after she had escaped from her master. Kat was trying desperately to find a way out of the makeshift arena the men on horses had created by totally surrounding her. By now, most of them were drunk, as they had been passing around a couple of whiskey bottles. They continued to taunt and grope her. Every time she broke loose from the grip of one White man who wasn't on horseback, another would grab her, ripping her dress more each time in the process. Her dress now looked like a collection of rags, barely stitched together.

Kat was a realist; she knew she was on the brink of being murdered. "If I have to die, please let them kill me now, before they rape me," she thought, seeing murder and carnal lust in her attacker's eyes.

They planned to rape her before they killed her. Not knowing Jesus Christ, she presumed her only salvation was quick death.

Without warning to her attackers, Kat snatched a gun out of the holster of one of her drunken tormentors. She had never touched a gun before, let alone waved one in someone's face. So, upon seizing the steel weapon, the sheer weight of it surprised her. The gun went from being parallel to the ground to almost perpendicular as it weighed down her arm. This brought about a round of laughter from her attackers. Grasping the gun with both hands, she recovered quickly. This time, she brought the laughter to an abrupt halt.

Wielding the gun with reckless abandon, she managed to back down most of her attackers. Though it seemed effective, she had made a tactical error. Paralyzing pain beset both arms as she found herself being lifted off the ground, from behind. She dropped the gun instantly. The thud produced by the gun hitting the hard ground was lost as the laughter from her attackers started again.

Jake, who was the biggest of the men, stood 6 feet 11 inches tall and weighed over six, fifty-pound grain sacks -- mostly solid muscle. When Jake picked up Kat, he was not gentle with her, restricting her blood circulation with his mighty grip. The tormenting pain in her arms pushed Kat to the edge of consciousness.

Bill, Julian, Rusty, Ham, Ricochet, and Cliff had been watching in disbelief. Luckily the slave catchers didn't hear the time traveler's hot debate. Two sides formed quickly; Ricochet, Ham, Cliff and Rusty were set against the two scientists. Morally, Julian wanted to help the woman. Professionally, he knew he shouldn't. As a scientist he knew without question he shouldn't do anything that could change the course of history. However, of the four, Ricochet argued with the most passion as though driven to help this woman.

"It's a mistake that we are even here," Bill argued, "If we do any thing to upset the time line it could cause irreparable damage to the future. Besides, it's our duty not to interfere. All of this is a part of history and would have happened if we weren't here. As a matter of fact, it did already happen in our past."

Flowing over with contempt for the scientist, Ricochet said, "Who the heck do you think you are? Captain Picard, from the Enterprise? We don't have no 'Prime Directive.' The fact is, we are here, and she needs our help!" Saying that, he turned and stormed toward Kat and her attackers, not considering the repercussions of his harum-scarum actions.

Bill now changed his argument. He placed a hand gently on Julian's shoulder, saying, "We just can't leave him out there. He's an unarmed Black man running into the middle of a gang rape in the 19th century. What do you think they will do to him? He'd have a better chance if he were to walk into the middle of a KKK rally and ask, 'Where are the White women?' We *have* to do something to help him."

"Where are our guns? Rusty demanded."

A lump developed in Julian's throat. "I hid them way back there. I was afraid you guys might try to take them."

"You fool!" Cliff said, turning to run for the guns.

But Rusty stopped him. "No time, we've got to make this work now. We've got two pistols, two machetes, and a rope."

Rusty deployed everyone so they would surround the rape gang, while minimizing the possibility of getting hit by friendly fire. Rusty was paired with Ham; Cliff with Bill, and Julian was by himself. "Wait for my lead. We'll try to get the woman and Ricochet in the clear first. Don't shoot unless I shoot!" emphasized Rusty.

Sweat rolled down the center of Ricochet's back like steel ball bearings on a marble surface. He was unsure of whether this was caused by the high humidity that day or from the nervousness of doing the stupidest thing he had ever done in his life. Being an unarmed Black man and running right into the middle of a dozen mounted and heavily-armed White men was not exactly the smartest or healthiest thing to do. This course of action was not exactly what he had in mind when he foolishly left the safety of the brush. Though very intelligent, he allowed his emotions to back his brain into a corner this time, as he had about 200 yards to come up with a plan.

Jake held Kat high above his head. Turning, he showed her off like she was a cheap bowling trophy. She was feeling slight vertigo from the human gyroscopic display, but she suddenly found the strength to kick her attacker in the ribs. First, there was a quick escape of air from Jake's mouth. Then his eyes turned a deep blood-red color. "You witch," he said, struggling to get the words out. But he never lost his grip on her. Instead, he increased it. He started shaking her, as if she were a small rag doll.

This brought about more laughter from the crowd of men. Jake flung her to the ground. There was a heavy thud and rise of a small dust cloud as Kat's small frame bounced off of the hard dry ground. She cradled and clawed the ground slowly, trying to raise herself onto all four limbs. Although she had wanted to die earlier, her instincts made her grasp for life. Jake spat on her and shoved her to the ground with his foot. Any attempt to stand erect was lost as she again collapsed violently onto the hard ground. This brought about more cheers and laughter.

Jake reached down and ripped her dress more. Seeing more of her golden naturally tanned body brought about an even louder round of applause and cheers from the rest of the attackers. As the cheers subsided, someone in the crowd suggested loudly, "Hey, let's let Junior have a crack at it first." All heads turned toward three of the attackers who were still mounted on their horses. Two of them appeared to be in their teens, and the other appeared to be a man in his fifties. Two of the three turned to observe the third mounted horseman, who didn't really appear to be a man at all. He looked to be no more than 15 years old. Freckles and pockmarks covered every bit of his "Deliverance Banjo Player" looking face, which was not too far from the truth; Jake was actually his father and his uncle.

Junior developed a large enough grin to display several missing and blackened teeth. He dismounted his horse, almost falling in his haste, getting his foot caught in the stirrup.

The red evening sun was setting behind Junior. Through the crowd he swaggered, toward Kat, receiving pats of encouragement as he parted the crowd.

The woman opened her eyes to find Junior standing right over her, fumbling with the knotted rope that held up his pants. Showing his teeth, he grinned, causing Kat to almost vomit.

"My massa, Simon Winters will kill all yaw fo' dis," Kat yelled. The men froze. Simon Winters was a rich and powerful man who owned many slaves, all women. One by one some of the men started tugging at the reins on their horses. Kicking the animals in the sides with their spurred boots, they turned and rode off, toward town, until only Jake, Junior, and four others remained.

"Hey, where yaw going? What yaw 'fraid of Simon Winters for? I kin take care of him," Jake yelled, over the neighing horses and their clamoring hooves, to the retreating men. They didn't respond or even look back. They just disappeared over the horizon.

Kat struggled. She tried to move her arms but found Jake pinning them down to the ground, over her head. She screamed. The pitch and amplitude were so deafening that Junior immediately stopped fidgeting with his pants to cover his ears. Suddenly, Kat kicked Junior in the groin area, collapsing him in pain.

Now, Jake had had enough of Kat. He released one of her arms and drew back his fist to strike her in the face. Preparing herself for death, Kat looked up.

"HEEEEY!" Ricochet yelled, while still in a full sprint. Jake stopped his punch in midair. Everyone, including Kat, looked back into the bright setting sun, which was in the direction of this new voice. As Ricochet got within view of them he saw multiple expressions on their faces. Then he saw those expressions go from lust directly to hatred.

"Who in da world are you, boy? What in da world do you want? Look-ee here we got us another Negro." These were among the less derogative remarks Ricochet heard as he slowed his approach toward the circle of evil.

Trying to catch his breath, he was thinking and hoping this should be about the time his friends would come rushing from the woods to save him. As the men slowly advanced toward him, Ricochet had the undivided attention of all the slave catchers.

Being raised in a rough part of Detroit, he was no stranger to being surrounded by hostile people wanting to cause him bodily harm. He had learned running your mouth could sometimes get you into trouble. However, he also had learned, used correctly, your mouth could get you out of just as much trouble.

Speaking boldly, he waved and smiled, "How yaw doin? Whew! Dat run was longer dan I thought. My massa and fitty mo' men with guns are in da trees." He bent at the waist and slightly at knees. Then Ricochet placed his hands upon his knees to catch his breath. Straightening up as he finished his sentence, he pointed in a general westerly direction. "Dey're Chriss-tans and dey don't like what yaw doing up here. Dey was goin' to come out and kill all yaw for your sins. But, I begged dem not to shed any blood. So, my massa said, if I could git yaw to stop and let da woman go, dey wouldn't kill yaw."

"What in the world are ya talkin' bout, boy?" one of the men said, squinting and attempting to shield his eyes from the glaring red sun. "I dunt see nobody out dere. You come a runnin' up here and 'spect us to lissen to your colored behind. Now how do you 'spose you can make us stop?"

"Good question," Ricochet thought, hoping his people would now charge out and be the answer. Then, realizing the distance he traversed, he knew it would take them a few minutes to arrive.

The cool sweat beads rolling down his back increased and he could feel his body shaking slightly as the men inched closer toward him. But, he was a master at playing poker. He stared into the core of men, boldly making things up as he went along. Turning to look directly at Jake, Ricochet answered, "I figured I would fight your best guy. If he wins, den you can go on as you please. If I win, den you let the woman go, unharmed. Deal?"

A short dead silence fell upon this concentrated gathering as the slave catchers thought about it. Then, one of the older men spoke up. "Wait. Let's git dis scraight. Little, scrawny you *wunt* to fight Big Jake?" Ricochet nodded in agreement. "Okay, suit yur-self, boy. It's yur fune-ral. An by da way, where you learn to talk like dat, all propa an all?"

"Never mind that, Ricochet replied, "But why don't you jist let her go now? She won't git far. If I lose you can git her back."

"Whatsa matter, you don't truss us, boy?" Jake asked.

"No. I wouldn't trust you if you told me my left butt cheek looked like my right butt cheek." Ricochet muttered, undiscernibly.

"What'd you say, Boy?" one of slave hunters demanded.

Jake expelled, as he lifted the weight of his large body off his knees. Walking confidently toward Ricochet, he stepped over Kat, keeping an eye on her dangerous feet. Then looking back at her, he seductively stuck out his tongue. "I'll be back for you, buttercup," He said. Again, the slave catchers laughed and cheered.

A look of disgust washed over Kat's face. She spat toward him. Again, a round of laughter was heard from her drunken attackers.

Jake outweighed Ricochet by more than a hundred pounds but Kat believed her new hero had a chance. One thing she knew was Black men. Although typically, they weren't as heavy as their white counterparts, perhaps because they weren't fed as much, but pound for pound they were a lot stronger. She never understood how her people ever became enslaved with the strength they had.

Jake stood there, cracking his knuckles in preparation for the fight. Ricochet removed his jump suit. That left him with a pair of trousers and no shirt. The two men stood about five feet apart waiting for the bout to begin. The contrast between them was striking. Jake was very white and Ricochet, very dark. Jake was very tall and Ricochet was nearly a foot shorter. Jake weighed 320 pounds and Ricochet weighed 190 pounds. Jake carried more fat around the mid-section, where Ricochet had a dark rock-hard, washboard abdomen.

Everyone, including Kat looked on in anticipation of this bout. They had temporarily forgotten about the events of just a few moments earlier. Even Junior had forgotten about his pain and like an evolved ape, went through each illustrated stage, and now stood erect.

Meanwhile, within the cover of the thicket, Rusty took aim. Being a marksman, he was sure he could take Jake out from that distance.

"Not now," said Ham, pushing Rusty's gun to the ground.

"What are you doing?" Rusty demanded, "He's going to get killed out there!"

"Not to worry, let him have his fun first," responded Ham, confidently.

"Not to Worry?" Rusty questioned

"Trust me. Besides, he'll buy us an extra few minutes to get closer in the trees before we come out in the open. That way it'll be easier to surprise them. Then, this just might work." Ham assured.

One of the mounted horsemen tossed a dusty cowboy hat onto the ground between Jake and Ricochet, signifying the fight had started. Jake took on a stance with a left foot lead, both fists clinched and palms facing up. Ricochet assumed a Korean back stance. Jake circled Ricochet, looking for an opening to throw the first punch. Jake's arms were big as tree branches. If Ricochet's punches weren't accurate, they wouldn't be effective; Jake would demolish him.

Before Jake could launch a punch, Ricochet jumped straight up and delivered a snap kick to his nose. In pain, Jake brought his hand to his nose. When he removed it, blood streamed from his nose. Ricochet quickly followed with a series of alternating inside punches to Jake's solar plexus. All his punches and kicks were accompanied by loud yells. Next, he delivered a punch to each eye and an open knife hand to the throat. Gasping for air, Jake grabbed his throat. However, Ricochet was not through with his first barrage.

The next kick was a back kick to Jake's abdomen. This was enough to bend Jake at the waist. Taking advantage of this position, Ricochet spun and faced his opponent once again, dropping him to the ground with an axe kick to the back of his head. There was a heavy thud as Jake hit the ground.

"Git up, Jake. Dunt let no darkee do dat to ya."
Pushing himself onto all four limbs, Jake gasped to get air into his lungs, coughing up blood and mucous. Kat had never in her life seen a Colored man *whip up* on a White man before. Especially like that.

"Wat type of fightin is dis, where you use yo' feet?" she thought. The more she saw of this Colored man, the more of a mystery he was to her.

Jake finally got to his feet again, blood still spewing from his nose. He approached Ricochet, now throwing punches more defensively than offensively. He threw a left cross but Ricochet sidestepped and countered with three lighting-fast roundhouse kicks to the ribs. Spinning to get behind him, Ricochet sent a sidekick to Jake's back. This, the most powerful kick in Ricochet's arsenal, sent Jake onto the ground, face down in the dirt, apparently defeated. However, unbeknownst to Ricochet, Jake had picked up two fistfuls of dirt while he was on the ground.

Getting up like a punch-drunk fighter, he snarled, "I'm gonna kick your butt, Black Boy." Lunging toward Ricochet, he faked a punch and threw the dirt. Ricochet winced and quickly brought his hands to his face, trying to rub the dirt out of his eyes.

Seizing the opportunity, Jake lunged toward Ricochet, driving him backward into a horse. They both fell under the horse, startling it. It reared, striking Ricochet in the forehead with a hoof. The wound spewed blood and painted his face red. Seeing this, the other time travelers hurried their pace, trying to get to a close position so the element of surprise would be on their side. But the element of surprise would not do them any good if Ricochet were dead when they got there.

Ricochet tried to focus but he now saw multiple images of Jake. Jake pulled him to his feet, hitting him twice, once in the liver. Then he picked him up and slammed him to the ground.

The multiple images of Jake were now reduced to just three. Opening his eyes, Ricochet saw the bottom of three separate boots hovering over him, ready to crush his face. Reflexively, he rolled out of the way and got to his feet. Now, he saw three Jakes standing before him. Ricochet had to make a choice as to which Jake to hit. He chose the one in the middle.

He steadied himself just long enough to jump and deliver with his right foot, a front snap kick to the head of the Jake in the middle. This time it was blocked by one of Jake's massive arms, causing Ricochet's foot to rivet with pain from the contact. Landing back onto the ground, Ricochet staggered. He tried the snap kick again, only this time he faked with his right foot then doubled with his left. He felt a direct hit from the second kick, as his foot made contact with Jake's nose again. Feeling the nose crumble under his foot, he was sure he had broken it.

Still concentrating on the Jake in the middle, Ricochet unleashed ten successive punches to Jake's solar plexus and abdomen. Jake stumbled backward. This was the first time he had moved backward doing the whole fight.

Ricochet landed three successive hook kicks to the side of Jake's face. Six feet tall or seven feet tall, two hundred pounds or three hundred pounds, this was just too much punishment for anybody to take. Ricochet didn't know if it was because his head was still ringing, but he thought he could hear the Spotted Owls searching for a new home as Jake was felled like a giant redwood. Jake had barely hit the ground, nor had Ricochet been able to clear his vision when he heard the sounds of protest.

"Boy!" Ricochet somehow expected to hear that and a lot worse. What he didn't expect was the feeling of hot lead in his shoulder. He heard the shot, and then immediately felt the searing pain of hot metal entering his body. It didn't matter who fired the shot, as all of the slave catchers had the same satisfying look, which simply expressed, "If he didn't do it, I would have."

Suddenly, there were multiple shots fired from the wooded area at close range. Bill threw a machete at one of the men. Impaling his chest, he fell to the ground, creating a small dust cloud. Not sure of what to aim at, some of the slave catchers fired back into the woods. There was mass confusion as they ducked while frantically looking about in every direction, trying desperately to avoid becoming victims of this attack.

But the Time Team was very organized. They worked well together, like an assembly line. Ham and Bill took advantage of the sudden bedlam. Ham charged into the ruckus, wielding his machete with the prowess of a medieval knight. He slashed one of the slave catchers across the throat with his machete. The man dropped his gun and quickly grabbed his throat, trying, in a feeble attempt, to keep his blood and his life from spilling onto the earth. Soon, falling face-forward to the ground, he lost that battle.

Now unimpeded, Ham made his way toward a mounted slave catcher who was firing wildly into the woods. Running, he thrust the machete through the horseman's thigh and downward into the horse's back. The man screamed out and the horse staggered, causing its rider to fall from the saddle yet still remain pinned to the horse's side. As the horse fell to the ground, it crushed its rider, ceasing the screaming and the pain.

Bill had darted in and began dragging Ricochet out by his legs. But he was delayed as a slave catcher grabbed him. They wrestled. Junior and his teenage friend decided they wanted no part of this. He quickly mounted his horse and rode away fast, following his friend who had never gotten off his horse. They started up the path that had earlier led them to the clearing. But unbeknownst to them, Julian had tied a rope around a tree on one side of the path and laid it on the ground, wrapping the other end around a tree on the other side of the path. As the lead rider approached, he pulled the rope tight. Immediately, the horse tripped. Toppling end over end, it threw the rider, causing him to topple end over end, also. Seeing this unfold in front of him, Junior spurred his horse, commanding it to leap over the rope. Once clear of the obstacle, he rode hard and swiftly toward freedom, never looking back. Julian ran to the unmoving grounded rider and checked him. His face was covered with sweat and red dirt; blood trickled from his nose while his head and neck were   skewed abnormally. His neck was broke. But, his horse had faired much better from the fall. It up-righted itself and stood by the side of the path. Going to it, Julian removed the rifle stowed in a holster on the saddle. Turning, he ran to help the other time travelers.

Rusty gunned down another slave catcher. He saw Bill and a slave catcher fighting for possession of a gun. He aimed but couldn't get a good aim on his target so he waited for an opening.

Kat knew she had to get out of the direct line of fire. She turned to run but was scooped up, quickly. Kat protested, wildly, as Cliff slung her over his shoulder and dashed for the wooded covering. Suddenly, a sharp pain shot down his back. His knees buckled, slightly. He thought he was shot then realized the woman's fingernails caused the pain. Punching and clawing at the small of his back, Kat continued to fight her rescuer.

"Hey, I here to help you," Cliff yelled, over his shoulder. Although this did not stop her, it did slow down her punches while she briefly contemplated his words.

Bill, still in a struggle with the last slave catcher, dropped to one knee after receiving a solid punch to his abdomen. His opponent quickly snatched his gun from the ground. He aimed. But, he too fell to the ground after not one, but two shots were fired from Rusty and Julian. Then, it ended.

CHAPTER 4

*Kat wiped away the dry blood from the wound in Ricochet's upper-*chest and shoulder area, and sponged the sweat from his brow. He had developed a fever. The bullet lodged in his upper-chest would require medical attention as soon as possible.

Ricochet was laid in the bedroom of the old farmhouse where they had regrouped. Kat tried looking away but often found she was staring at the hard chest and abdominal muscles of this man who had risked his life to save her. His chest was dark, chiseled and flawless except for the bullet wound. But, upon hearing the men in the other room, Kat's attention was suddenly diverted.

"I say we just leave her here. She already got my friend shot-up. I tell you, I can smell trouble, and she's nothing but trouble. Women are nothing but trouble in any century," she heard the one called Ham say.

"We just can't leave her here," said Cliff.

"And why not? We don't need her to get back," retorted Ham.

"You know as well as I do, if we leave her here, she's as good as dead," answered Julian, glaring at Ham. Kat wanted badly to see into the room where these men were arguing and discussing her fate without her. But feared pushing the door open any further, thinking she would be discovered.

Ham was greatly outnumbered but he wasn't quite ready to give up yet. "If we hadn't shown up to rescue her, she'd probably be dead anyway. You were the one yappin' about the time line. So, if she's supposed to be dead, then let her die. She's the reason my best friend is in there right now, dying." Pointing toward the back bedroom, Ham continued. "What we need to do is leave *her* butt here and get *our* butts on that stupid Time Machine. And get back to the future so we can get Ricochet to a hospital."

85

The debate went back and forth for another ten minutes. Kat continued to press herself hard against the bedroom door, listening to every word of the argument. Finally she heard the one who was called Julian, say, "Enough! I'm in charge here and I've made up our minds! As long as we are in for a penny, we might as well be in for a pound! We're *not* going to let her die!"

The time travelers brought Kat into the main room and began to explain the situation to her: about how they were time travelers from the future. After a few seconds, she felt a chill permeate her body.

Turning, she found a pair of scrutinizing eyes so full of hatred they were red. From what she had heard earlier, she knew right away these eyes belonged to the man they called Ham. Kat allowed them to finish uninterrupted.

"Is there anywhere we can take you where you would be safe?" Julian asked. She looked Ham directly in his eyes and smiled. She knew she had done nothing wrong. Although he hated her, she wasn't going to trade evil for evil.

She didn't know where she had heard it from, but Kat lived by a biblical standard, which read, "If I love you more, will you love me less?"

Kat explained she was a slave and the men who were after her were slave bounty hunters, who didn't mind bringing her back dead or alive. They got paid just the same. Most of the slave masters would rather have a live slave. But, a dead slave was just as valuable, as they became excellent examples to any other slaves contemplating escape. After she explained this to them she told them where they could take her.

"Dares a train leevin' un da unda—groun rai-road leevin tamaro mo-nin' for up-nort. The *Black Moses* is takin' slaves to be free. She's goin' up-nort to a place called Au--burn. Den weez goin' to Can-na-dah. To meet da train, dats where I wuz on my way to when dey caught me. It's 'bout a hour ride from here."

"You mean you want us to take you to a place an hour from here?" Ham interrupted, "Look, we saved your life. What else do want us to do, baby-sit you? What's the matter, slave work too hard for your candy-butt? Or are you just too good to get out in the field with the rest of the slaves?" Ham mocked. "You're probably a house slave, ain't you?" If Kat had been a few shades darker there wouldn't have been any telltale signs of the anger that had quickly come to a head. However, as it was, her face turned bright orange.

"You don't know nuttin' 'bout me!" she rebutted, "You got no right to judge me, no matta what anyone says. I'll neva believe dat anyone is betta din me. If you mus' know, I wuz a slave, workin' in da fiels, and all I ever wanted wuz to be free. I wuznt runnin away frum workin in da fiel', at least not dis time. At furs' I wuz working on Massa Tom Chambers plan—tay-chun. The work in da fiels was real hard, but my husban' made me forget 'bout my trou-boze."

Kat took a deep breath. Reminiscing and collecting herself, she continued. "My husban, Toby wuz always talkin' 'bout free-dom, an' how one day he would take me to a place betta dan dis, a place where everyone wuz free, even colored folks. He said dat chains wuzn't right for colored folks. Den I got preg-nut. Dis only made Toby talk mo' bout free-dom. He kep' sayin' how he wanted our chillens to be born free human-beins'. Den one night when I wuz still only 'bout three munts preg-nut, Toby said dat we needed to git to bed early , wit' all our clothes on. He woke me a few hours lata and said dat we wuz leavin on da unda—groun railroad. At firs' I didn' tink dat da white folks would let us ride on da trains. Later, when we lef', he 'splained the whole thing to me. But dat wuz da las time we talked."

"Dey cawt us dat night. Da slave—huntas killed Toby, and brawt me back. When I got back to my massa, he beat me; he beat me real hard. I loss my Toby, my baby, and any care I had 'bout life in one long night."

In tears by now, Kat had everyone's undivided attention, including Ham's. Composing herself again, she continued. "Masser Chambers kep' me 'round fur about three mo' months. Den he said dat I was no good to him no mo'. He sold me to a man named Simon Winters.

"I should known somethin' wuz wrong when he came to buy me. Dey undressed me, but dey didn't look at me like to see 'ow much work I could do. Dey looked at me mo' dif-fer-ent. I 'member Massa Winters paid a lower price cuz of my whip marks. Massa Winters had thirty slaves--all girls. He didn't own a plan-ta-chun, jist two big houses. We wuz slave pos-ti-toots. I didn't even know what dat wuz til I wuz called dat, and a whole lot of utter names. Men come from all over da' county to see Massa Winter's girls

"Once I started working dare I started not likin' myself no mo'. I knowed we wuz all Massa Winter's slaves, but dis was even worser den bein' a slave. At furs' I wanted ta kill myself, wit' all dem mens touchin' and taking liberties wiff me. Den I decided to 'scape and hope dat dey would kill me if dey caught me. It took me less dan a week 'fo I could figure out a plan."

"I wuz on my way to meet a con-duk-tor on the unda-groun railroad. We wuz going to Ca-na-da. Dat's when dey caught me, fo' I could git to da railroad." Kat's eyes began to turn red as the tears filled the wells of her eyes. The men stood in silence as the ambient light and tears accented Kat's beauty. There was no eye make-up or mascara to pollute the tracks of tears on her face; they were sparkling and clear.

Kat stood five-feet-seven inches tall. She was slim but had a figure her baggy slave clothing did not conceal very well. The dim oil lamp flickered and refracted off one of her tears, producing an array of colors falling from her cinnamon colored face. Each man in the room thought the exact same thing, she was truly beautiful. Taking a brief pause, Kat changed the subject quickly, as if to hide the fact that she had been crying at all.

"I hope dat Ricochet's okay. I ain't never 'ad no man stan' up and fight fur me before," Kat said. She wiped the last remnants of tears from her face and went into the bedroom to administer to Ricochet. She found him still unconscious. He had lost a lot of blood. But when she rubbed his forehead and chest, she found his fever had decreased somewhat. And it appeared to her, even though he was still unconscious, his body responded to her touch. She could not explain how; she could only sense it. Her hand now lay upon Ricochet's chest. Just then, Ham entered the room, startling her as he walked up to her from behind.

"What's up with him?" Ham asked. Kat jumped and clutched toward her heart.

"Mercy, you scared me outa my wits."

"Sorry," Ham replied. "I just wanted to check on him." He paused. "And, also to apologize to you. You know, we learned about slavery in the future but it was one-dimensional. We were never taught that our sisters were slave-prostitutes. We just automatically assumed all the slaves were on plantations."

"You mean dat in da future dars nomo' slav'ry?" Kat asked.

"No, not really," Ham answered, with some reservation, thinking of the discrimination that still plagued the 21st century.

Kat pondered this for a second or two then said, "Tell me den. When are wees goin' ta be free?"

Smiling, and with his best Jesse Jackson impersonation, Ham answered, "How long? Not long."

Darkness fell until the only light illuminating the room was from a tiny oil lamp. Ham had noticed the way Kat was caring for Ricochet. It was a little more than he would expect. True, he had saved her life. And he was hurt bad. Yet, Ham could tell she was falling in love with his best friend.

"You know this isn't the first time he has done something like this. When we were seventeen, in high school, he did almost the exact same thing," Ham announced.

With wide eyes, Kat looked at Ham, interjecting, "Dey let colared folks go to school in da fu-chur

Ham smiled, then continued, "I remember it well . . . . It was at Cass Technical High School in Detroit. I was on the fourth floor by Mr. Down's and Mr. Miller's Electronics Lab. And I was fighting this guy. I was winning, but his nine buddies had me surrounded and were just about to jump me. Three or four of them had knives. Cass is a very prestigious school, where the very intelligent students go. But intelligent or not, boys will be boys. Thus, knives in the school were not that uncommon.

"Apparently, Ricochet, with his girlfriend was just walking down the stairs from the fifth floor. So he was able to see over the crowd. When he saw what was happening, he left his girlfriend behind. Let's see...what was her name? Oh, Mary Kampbell, that's right. I wonder what ever happened to her? Ricochet really loved her. Well anyway, Ricochet flew down the stairs, burst through the crowd and grabbed the biggest guy. After that it turned into a big ruckus. It actually ended up being four against ten because two more of Ricochet's friends joined in: Dimitrious, a big Greek guy, and Captain Ash."

Ham smiled, recollecting the next thing he said. "Old Captain Ash. His real name was Mick Davis. But he never used any lotion, so we always called him Captain Ash. In fact, whenever he did put lotion on, it would jump off his skin. I think his birthday is actually on Ash Wednesday. Anyway, to make a short story shorter, we won the fight. And Ricochet and I became tighter through the years. That's why I love this guy."

"You forgot to tell her about the time we got drunk and you were hanging out of my car puking. 'Frank-eeee, roll the window back up!'" Ricochet interjected, groggily but cheerfully. Then he and Ham laughed together. It was an inside joke. Ham told Kat he would explain it to her later. She gave a sheepish consolatory laugh. She was just happy to see him finally wake up. "Did I miss much?" Ricochet asked. "Where's that big gumpy dude I was fighting?"

"He's dead, all of them, except one got away." Ham replied. Ricochet cursed. Then he realized he was in the presence of a lady, so he apologized. He rephrased it,

"Dang, I was hoping that big, Gerry Cooney-looking guy was still around. I felt like Larry Holmes whuppin' up on him. Hey, Ham, did you see the way I broke him down?"

Ham laughed, saying, "Man, you really kicked his butt. You broke him down so hard the Maytag repairman got the Holy Ghost. You were on his butt like a pair of super-glued Fruit of the Looms." Both burst into loud laughter, only to be interrupted by Ricochet's wheezing and gasping. At that moment, Rusty and Julian entered the room.

"Welcome back. I'm glad to see you're feeling better," Julian said. While checking Ricochet's condition, Julian and Ham informed him of the latest plan. That plan was for Rusty and Bill to take Kat to the Underground Railroad early in the morning, before dawn. They were to take three of the horses they got from the slave catchers. Rusty and Bill were chosen because they were the only two in the group who knew how to ride a horse. Also, if they were stopped on the way, they could easily pose as her masters. "Can you ride a horse?" Julian asked Kat. She nodded. He then instructed Ham to take the first watch.

As Julian, Rusty and Ham left the room, Rusty turned, saying to Ricochet, "I just want to tell you, that was one of the bravest things I've ever seen. Out there, when you took up for the lady. It was also one of the stupidest things I've seen. Nevertheless, it was the bravest. Besides, I've done a few stupid things in my day. The police force could use a few good men like you."

Nodding his head in acknowledgment, Ricochet struggled, saying, "Yeah, well thanks for backing me up." He knew this was the closest he was going to get to an "at-a-boy" from a man who had tried to kill him just hours earlier.

There was a small cot in the bedroom, apparently, at one time used for a child, but with a little effort Kat could fit on it. Besides it was much better than sleeping on the cold floor. There was plenty of oil in the lamp so Kat decided to leave it on so she could keep an eye on her patient.

She had managed to stop most of the bleeding but Ricochet had still lost a lot of blood and was now shivering. She had previously looked around for a blanket for him but there was not one to be found in the whole house. The flickering flame and the exaggerated size of his shadow amplified the shivering. Feeling she had to do something about it, she climbed into bed with him, wrapping herself around him. She was careful not to disturb the makeshift bandages she had placed on his shoulder wound.

Kat had been through so much. And had lost so much in her lifetime. When she wrapped herself around Ricochet, yes, it was to keep him warm, but she desired something, also. But, she was not looking for a sexual experience. She couldn't give herself to that now. Perhaps, not ever again. She merely desired something to hang onto in her life, something that wouldn't hurt her, no matter how temporary it was. She could feel that in Ricochet. He would never hurt her. With intense warmness, she felt this in her heart. At this point in Kat's life, this feeling of never being hurt by someone was much better than love, and far exceeded any physical feelings from love. But even deeper in her heart, which she could not realize now because of all the hurt and loss she had experienced and felt, she felt one day she could love Ricochet, and in return he could love her.

"What your real name?" she asked.

No one had asked Ricochet for his real name in so long he actually drew a blank for a moment. "Bryan," he said after a short hesitation. He repeated the question to her.

"Kathleen," she answered, eagerly.

They talked for an hour before Ricochet had fallen asleep. Although Kat did most of the talking, they had shared enough intimate knowledge about each other to be able to fall in love. All they now needed was time, time together. Ironically, the Time Machine could not do that for them now. In fact, before he went to sleep Ricochet was contemplating how he could bring her back to the future with him.

The accumulation of the day's events finally caught up with him; he fell into a hard but peaceful sleep. His last thoughts were of Kat before he fell asleep. "I wish you could come back to the future with me," He thought.

A few minutes later, first making sure he was asleep, Kat kissed him on his cheek, saying, "I wish you could stay here wit' me."

*****

It was almost dawn when they left: Bill, Rusty and Kat. And it had been an hour's ride, just as Kat had said. The hard part was going to be finding their way back.

It had been a good ride. However, only the initial time of riding a horse is good when one rides for an hour straight after one hasn't ridden a horse in years. It had been a long time since Rusty had ridden a horse. He quickly got used to it, though age and lack of exercise were making the ride more painful than it should have been. Bill was faring well. Before Bill had come to America, he had belonged to a hunting club in France where they rode for the foxhunt.

"Do you think she'll be alright?" Bill asked, breaking the verbal silence and the hypnotic clamor of the horse's hooves, "I mean, do you think she will make it to freedom?"

"Of course she will," Rusty replied. "Do you know who that was back there, the conductor?" When they left Kat with the small group of runaway slaves on the Underground Railroad, the conductor never gave her name but Rusty overheard someone call her *Moses*. But even before that, he recognized her from her photos in the history books. Earlier, he had the same concern about Kat's safety as Bill had.

"That, my friend, was the one and only Harriet Tubman. They've got a long, hard, and dangerous journey ahead of them. To reach Canada, they've got to go though Wilmington, Delaware and Philadelphia. And even though Pennsylvania is a free state, the US government still considers the slaves to be property, making it legal for bounty slave catchers, like the ones we encountered yesterday, to bring them back to a slave state. But the way history reports it, she never got caught, nor did she ever lose a passenger. In fact, if along the way, a passenger got scared and wanted to turn back, Harriet Tubman, knowing this would risk the whole train's safety, would pull out a pistol and say, 'You'll be free or you'll die a slave.' I think they will make it. If I wasn't sure I wouldn't have left her there."

"Why do you care so much that she makes it?" Bill asked, "I care, but you seem to be more driven. And how do you know so much detail about African-American history? I bet eighty percent of Africans-Americans don't know those facts, especially the Underground Railroad route. Are you part African-American?

"No, I don't think I am. I just know. I know because I care. I care because I have been real close to African-Americans. I don't look at them as African-Americans, I look at them as friends." Rusty explained, reminiscing. It was going to be a long ride back and a story was exactly what they needed to pass the time away. So, Rusty shared his story.

*****

Growing up in the hills and mountains of Idaho, the only time Rusty had seen a Black man was when his father would sweep the chimney. So, Rusty's father had taught him everything he had known about Black people. But, long before Rusty had been born, his father lived in Los Angeles and married a woman who had run off with a Black man, leaving Rusty's father heart-broken and bitter. Then, he had moved to the mountains of Idaho to get away from Black people. There, he had married Rusty's mother, and there he had tried to bequeath to his son an inheritance of bitterness and hate.

Upon joining the police force in Los Angeles, years later, Rusty quickly discovered almost everything he had been taught about Black people while growing up in Idaho was wrong. And what wasn't wrong usually happened for a good reason. While on the force in Los Angeles he had forged strong friendships with African-Americans. In fact, his partner and best friend was a Black man.

Rob was very dark and very proud. His friends joked that he looked and acted much like the actor Wesley Snipes. Rusty would often tease Rob, calling him the Wesley Snipes of law enforcement. Rob would retort, "The darker the berry, the sweeter the juice."

To which Rusty would respond, "Yeah, but who wants diabetes?"

Rusty stood 6 feet 4 inches and weighed about 240 pounds. Yet, despite his hulking size he had a boyish face, covered with as many freckles as there were stars in the Milky Way. With his bright red, mop-like hair he was a ringer for a giant Opie Taylor.

His favorite type of music was disco from the '70s, especially KC and the Sunshine Band, Peter Brown, AWB, and Wild Cherry. "Play that funky music, big White boy," Rob would mutter whenever Rusty blasted his music in the patrol car.

But, Rusty lost his best friend and partner during a shootout in Los Angeles. He had always known he might lose a partner in the line of duty, but this was different. What really disturbed him was Rob had actually sacrificed his life so Rusty could live. Rusty blamed himself for years. He thought he should have died on that warm June day instead of Rob.

On the day Rob died, he had parked the police car on the third level of an outdoor parking garage so Rusty could take care of some business with his lawyer in an adjacent office building. As they exited the squad car, they saw a youth attempting to break into a vehicle. They chased him down the stairs, out of the garage and into a meat packing business directly across the street. Rob and Rusty had entered the building and conducted a thermal sweep, using the standard field issue Thermal Scanning Unit. The device showed only one person in the building. They had proceeded cautiously, and on the second story, found the youth. But a scuffle arose and in the process of arresting him, the suspect was inexplicably knocked unconscious. Rob had instructed Rusty to stay by the suspect, while he went across the street to get the squad car.

As soon as Rob left the building, from the freezer where they had been able to elude the TSU, three other gang members ambushed Rusty with automatic assault weapons. In the ensuing gunfight, Rusty had been able to hold his own for a few minutes, but realistically, he was completely out-gunned. He had sustained several gunshot wounds before he could crawl to safety behind some heavy refrigeration equipment, leaving long, bloody trails on the cement deck like an artist painting crimson strokes onto a gray canvas. Gurgling blood and gasping for air, he radioed Rob, frantically. "They've got me pinned down. I've been hit three times. I need backup now! I mean nnooooow!"

Rob received the call while on the third level of the garage, but he was still a good twenty to thirty yards from the squad car. He had two choices. He could run all the way down to the first level then cross the street to reach the building, or drive out of the garage in a downward spiral, hoping his progress would not be impeded by a slow driving motorist in the narrow one-way exit route. He struggled only briefly with this decision.

As he sprinted to the police car, a sudden high-pitched, shattering sound got his undivided attention. It was the sound of breaking glass. Looking out over the waist-high concrete barrier separating the third level lot from the street below, Rob could see a large window, after it had been riddled with bullets, almost completely shot out. Hearing more gunshots, he accelerated into a full sprint. Hurdling over a couple of parked cars, he danced across their hoods like a halfback pursuing a touchdown. He started the squad car and spun it around backwards, out of the parking spot. When he came to the far wall of the garage, he stopped and looked through the opening between the garage floor levels, toward the part of the building where Rusty was trapped. He also made a mental note of the 'EXIT' sign ahead on his right. Jamming his foot on the accelerator so hard, he cracked the floorboard of the police car. He felt and heard his ankle pop. Ignoring the pain, he accelerated quickly toward the exit turn, knowing there would be no way he could make such a tight turn at the speed he had already obtained.

Instead of slowing down, however, Rob continued to accelerate, straight toward the cement barrier. Instinctively, he closed his eyes so tight he squeezed tears from them. He crashed directly into the cement wall. When Rob opened his eyes he thought he might be waking up in a hospital bed; he was not there. Instead, he had crashed through the cement barrier and was now in mid-air praying to God that his *guestimation* of speed and distance were correct; they were. For the moment, God was with Rob.

As if an architect had drawn it, the police car launched from the third story of the garage in a perfect arch, flew across the narrow alley, and crashed directly into the large window on the second floor of the meat packing building.

What Rob had not figured was that the gang firing on his partner had positioned themselves with their backs toward that same window. Rusty, still firing back, was still pinned behind the refrigeration equipment. He was out-gunned and outnumbered three to one, wounded and losing blood rapidly. Compared with their nine shots, he was only able to get off two shots at a time. He was running out of ammunition faster than he was running out of blood. Loading his last rounds into his clip, Rusty peered out from behind the equipment. He saw something he knew could only be an illusion caused by his loss of blood: a flying car. And it was coming straight at him through the large shattered window.

Rusty's dilemma now was to discount the possible illusion and stay hidden behind the equipment or to try to roll out of the way while risking being shot again. Just as Rusty made his move, the police car barreled through what was left of the second story window.

God and timing saved Rusty's life. Just as he rolled into the open area, the fact that a two-ton police vehicle was about to crush them to death demanded the immediate and undivided attention of the gang members. Two of them were crushed instantly, their bodies mangled and dragged as the police car skidded, scraped and arced against the cement deck. As if being shot from a canon, the third and quickest gang member leapt out of the way, avoiding a violent death similar to that of his friends. But, the front quarter panel on the driver's side of the police car struck him. He lay in the rubble, semi-conscious and severely injured.

Landing the car, Rob said his very quick thanks to the Lord, mainly, for being on solid ground once again. Unaware of the extent of damage he had inflicted on the gang members, he did not want to stop the police car right in the middle of gunfire. Regaining control of the vehicle, he yanked the steering wheel and took a hard left turn, barely preventing the two-ton squad car from slamming headfirst into another cement wall.

With his rocky ride not quite over, Rob proceeded further for another twenty-five yards before he plowed into a wall of sides of beef hanging from the overhead. It was as if his life had been spared by forty soft, fat men, who were doing pull-ups from the ceiling.

Slightly stunned and with a leg that had snapped in two as soon as he crashed through the window, Rob dragged himself out of the car, unaware of two events unfolding. First, when he had crashed through the window, the gas tank on the police car ruptured and was now leaking profusely. Also, the gang member who had been injured earlier had quickly regained consciousness. Bloody, dirty, with parts of his body bent in abnormal positions, and looking like a jigsaw puzzle with a couple of pieces missing, the gang member was now making his way toward the police car. He carried an AK .47 in his left hand like a coiled serpent waiting to strike out as he stalked Rob. When he had Rob clearly in view, he raised his weapon, took aim, and snarled, "This is for my brothers! They were my only brothers!"

Rob, who had managed to drag himself out of the car, was sitting down, propped against the driver's side rear tire. Stunned, semi-paralyzed and bleeding profusely from the head, Rob managed to raise his head, and look his would-be murderer in the eyes. The look wasn't a look of fear, contempt, or hatred, but one of contentment as he prepared for the end.

A single shot rang out; Rob didn't flinch. But, it was not the rapid-fire sound he had expected to hear from the automatic assault weapon.

Collapsing to his knees, then falling forward, the would-be murderer's face fell unimpeded, striking the cement ground with a solid thud. Blood projected from his mouth, while buried deep within his brain was a 12-mm slug. A bullet-riddled Rusty stood behind him, barely able to stand erect, his handgun still smoking.

Yet, there was very little time to celebrate. Rob only managed to manufacture a half-smile before it changed to something that looked a lot more serious and horrifying.

As the gang member had collapsed onto the cement floor, his trigger finger still on the lever had activated the weapon. There was no immediate danger to Rob or Rusty; the gun was not directly aimed at either of them.

Within the dead man's tight grasp, the gun discharged loudly and powerfully, then leapt out of the shooter's hand and fell to the ground, still firing deadly bullets. The projecting hot flames from the gun barrel ignited a trail of gasoline leading to the police car.

Unable to move, Rob saw the blue and orange flames quickly making their way toward the gas tank and himself, like an athlete running the last leg of the course, carrying the hand torch to light the Olympic flame. Rob didn't have time to think or say goodbye with his voice. That would have required too many muscles to move that were not able to move, too many syllables to say, and cause too much pain in too little time. He said goodbye to his partner and best friend with his eyes.

The deafening explosion, the bright flash and a short glimpse of his partner burning to death was all Rusty could remember for some time after. But the next thing he did remember was waking in the hospital with bandages over most of his body.

*****

After Rusty had finished the story, Bill remained silent for a few seconds and then responded, "I understand. I'm sorry about your partner. But answer this for me?" He paused.

Looking Rusty directly into his eyes, Bill asked, "The car flying through the air, the sides of beef, tell me, was that story entirely true?"

Rusty found it hard to keep a straight face. With a crooked smile he answered, "Absolutely! Well, most of it is. Some of the facts were changed to protect the unimaginative," now grinning even more.

"It's a good thing we're riding horses instead of cattle," Bill volleyed.

"Why?" Rusty asked.

"Because, I'd hate to step in your bull-crap," Bill answered, laughing heartily.

The horses were under more strain to reach the top of the ridge than they had been when they had passed this spot earlier. Rusty and Bill had been riding the horses hard for over ninety minutes without water or rest, except for the short time it took to leave Kat with Harriet Tubman. When they reached the top of the ridge, Bill had finally convinced Rusty to rest the horses at a pond for ten minutes. Definitely in need of the stop, the horses drank like they were camels.

They had dropped Kat off thirty minutes prior and were well over half the way back to the farmhouse. The sun had begun to rise and they were now feeling the rising temperature on their backs and seeing a golden glow on everything in front of them. However, none of those things were as beautiful as the prism effect of the morning dew on the hillside as the sun refracted multiple colors off each dewdrop.

Though they had managed to bend and cheat time just some twelve linear hours ago, one might be inclined to think they had mastered it. However, ironic as it seemed, time was definitely a master rather than a slave to them now.

While Bill was watering the horses, Rusty walked to the edge of the ridge. He marveled at how good the land looked before man turned it into an urban concrete-jungle. Looking toward the east, he could see the rolling countryside for miles. The surface was still moist with dew. Again, Rusty was taken by the display of colors the dew and the amber sun displayed. Then, in the same direction he saw a patch of the colors disappear for a brief instant and then reappear. Then he saw it again, only, the patch was getting larger.

A lump began to form in Rusty's throat. He knew what was happening. It was what they had feared. It was a posse of killers coming for them. "If I could have only stopped that one slave catcher from escaping," he thought.

At the rate they were moving, Rusty determined the posse was maybe ten minutes behind them. Hastily, he ran to Bill, informing him they needed to ride out immediately. Rusty quickly swallowed a handful of water before they rode out at top speed, toward the farmhouse.

The farmhouse was only about thirty more minutes away. Barring any unforeseen occurrences, they would definitely get there before the posse. The hard part was to keep the posse from gaining any ground on them. Ten minutes was just barely enough time for the time travelers to get the Time Machine on line before the posse caught them, and that was pushing it.

The Time Machine would now be operating mostly off its Duracellium source; the small amount of light that entered the barn was not enough to drive the solar cells. Julian would have to wait until they arrived before he initiated the operating sequence. Bill knew they would only get one shot at it so he wanted to make sure it was a good one.

Like an old car in need of a new muffler, everyone in the farmhouse heard the sounds from the heavy panting of the horses and their hooves clamoring on the hard ground as they rode up to the farmhouse. A few seconds later, the front door exploded off its old rusty hinges. In his army-like police uniform, Rusty rushed in. "We got to get out of here now! There're probably about 25 of them, riding hard, and headed this way!" Rusty proclaimed. There was not a word or even a glance exchanged by anyone, only action followed. Everyone started gathering all of the equipment and gear, instantly.

"Make sure we get everything. We can't leave anything from the future here in the past, Julian instructed."

With his duffel bag slung over one shoulder, and with the help of Rusty, Ham picked up Ricochet who, responsively, groaned in agony from being moved so quickly. It was still morning. The sun was bright yellow and hot. But the silence in the immediate vicinity of the little farmhouse was broken by the sounds of five men running toward the barn and one man groaning in discomfort as he was carried. Julian was in the point position followed by Bill. Rusty and Ham, carrying Ricochet, were next, while Cliff brought up the rear.

Entering through the rickety, wooden, double-doors of the barn, they found the Time Machine covered with a white sheet, just as they had left it. Cliff, the last to enter through the barn door, stopped before he crossed the threshold, then stepped back. Silent and frozen in his tracks, he looked out over the horizon and saw nothing peculiar, but what he heard was enough to "flat-line" him.

It was again a clamor. But, not like the clamor produced by two horsemen, as before. This was much heavier, like rolling thunder. And from the increasing volume and vibrating ground, Cliff could tell it was rolling right toward them. In a few seconds, charging over the hillcrest, rode 25 heavily armed horsemen. At first they seemed to be heading toward the farmhouse, but as they spotted Cliff they abruptly changed course as easily as a swarm of locusts.

Cliff, who had never been considered a dumb cop, ran into the barn a little faster. He found the 'two by eight' board used for locking the barn door and put it into place. There were no windows in the barn on the first level, only on the second level, but sufficient sunlight shone through cracks and holes in the ceiling and walls. Because Ham had volunteered to help carry Ricochet, Cliff ended up with Ham's original duffel bag. Peering though a crack in the wall, he could see all of the horsemen. They were positioning themselves, but they were all in the open. Turning, Cliff could see Julian and Bill trying to start the Time Machine. Technically, he didn't know or understand what they were doing. However, he knew something wasn't right when he heard the word "problem."

"Hey, Darkies and Darky Lovers! We'll give ya just five seconds to come outta dere. Den we gonna blast ya out," yelled someone from outside the barn.

Cliff had a feeling five seconds wasn't going to be enough time for them to start the Time Machine and escape. Frantically, he reached into Ham's duffel bag. Small anxious sweat beads suddenly appeared on his forehead.

"One," bellowed a heavily armed horseman. By the time the countdown reached three, Cliff found what he was looking for. He quickly pulled out Ham's assault weapon, crowded the barrel through one of the sun cracks in the barn wall and aimed it right into the center of the mob of horsemen. Synchronously, with the countdown of four Cliff squeezed the trigger.

Terrified horses reared back and threw several riders to the ground. Delivering a rapid spraying of bullets, the single weapon dropped about three horsemen and horses, first to their knees, then to their deaths. The air was knit with the rapid, exploding sounds of the weapon, the neighing of horses screaming with fear and pain, and the heavy thuds of men and horses dropping to the ground. Unfortunately, since Cliff couldn't aim his gun through crack, most of the bullets didn't find targets, only air. He kept his finger on the trigger until the gun finally overheated and jammed.

Tossing the assault weapon aside, he reached for his side arm. He heard confusion outside the barn but he also heard a sweet sound from inside the barn. It was the sound of the Time Machine whirring to life and Julian announcing with jubilation, "That's it."

"COME ON!" Rusty yelled, motioning with his arm for Cliff to join them on the platform. The last thing Rusty wanted was to lose another partner.

The horsemen riddled the barn with bullets as soon as Cliff turned to run toward the platform. Bullets streaked through the air like miniature missiles causing wood splinters to fly about, saturating the air. The added rays of sunlight shone through the barn like lasers in a smoky room, as each lead bullet easily penetrated the flimsy wooden structure. Cliff dove for refuge behind a big metal anvil, disregarding the painful impact and the blood it drew as he butted his head squarely against the rusted metal. He made himself straight as an arrow and as narrow as a board to hide his entire body behind it.

Sparks flew off the front of the anvil as bullets struck it time and time again. Hearing and feeling the heat of a bullet whiz by his head, Julian yelled to Bill, "Get those shields up." The shields were instantly raised. There was a short shimmer of light along the perimeter when the shield came on line. They were now able to see just how close the bullets were coming to them. Sparks of amber light alerted them each time a bullet struck the shields. However, it wasn't the amber sparks of electricity that concerned them right now. It was the fact they were safe inside the shield, but Cliff wasn't.

Rusty saw his partner behind the anvil. He could see sparks fly off the anvil much like the shield of the time machine. "We just can't leave him out there!" he pleaded.

Spittle spewed forth from Julian's mouth as he yelled over the successive snapping and sizzling sounds of the bullets striking the shields. "I can't lower the shields now! We'll all be killed!" It looked like a Fourth of July fireworks display. "Besides, there's too much energy discharge. If I lower the shields now, we might not ever get them back up or the Time Machine started again." Julian added.

Behind the large anvil, Cliff could hear the sounds of the guns outside of the building, the wood of the shabbily constructed barn being perforated by bullets, and the high-pitched ping of the bullets hitting the anvil. Then a new sound joined the orchestra — the sound of glass shattering. Cliff turned to see what he really didn't want to see.

A lynch mob was outside trying to kill him. And the only thing between him and hundreds of bullets was an anvil. His only hope of getting out alive lay with the Time Machine; that same time machine was unreachable.

He saw a torch fly into the barn though the broken window on the second level. He thought, "Just when I thought things couldn't possibly get worse: the sky opened up and God said, 'I hate you Cliff.'"

Spreading quickly through the dry hay, the fire produced heavy, billowing smoke that filled the barn. Even if Cliff could get to the Time Machine through the gunshots, the fire had spread so quickly that it was too large for him to put out. Cliff now had two more enemies: smoke and fire. And he was separated from his only friends, who were safely behind an electronic force field. Grabbing a dirty white sheet from the ground, he used it as a filter to breathe through. The foul odor of old barn animal dung and urine saturated the sheet. But it was better than dying of smoke inhalation.

The thick near-toxic and acrid smoke burned his eyes. The stench of the sheet and the heat of the fire caused Cliff to experience a slight case of vertigo. Sweat poured from his forehead and rolled down his face.

At first, he was unable to detect the sudden absence of gunfire, and then he noticed. He reasoned that either everyone must be reloading their guns at the same time, or the lynch mob thought they had killed everyone. Cliff removed the sheet from his nose, wiped his brow and then looked at it. He had an idea. He knew he could buy himself some time, if he could just do it quickly. He tore the sheet and then cracked open the barn door. The thick black smoke billowed out of the barn door but the gunmen could still make out the simple pattern of a white flag of surrender being waved through the door.

"We're coming out!" Cliff yelled. "We just got to get our wounded." At first there was no response from outside of the barn. The only sound was that of crackling wood from the burning barn. Cliff hoped a non-answer was a positive answer. Then he heard a welcomed reply, finally, from outside of the barn.

"You got one minute boy!" came the response.

The sound of the force field deactivating was indeed a welcomed sound to Cliff. The fire had not spread to the time platform yet. Cliff could not see him though the smoke, but he heard Rusty urging him to hurry and get on the platform. Coughing as he ran through the thick black smoke, he followed the voice. Negotiating a small wall of fire and snatching up the duffel bag along the way, Cliff dashed toward the platform. There, Rusty grabbed him, jubilantly.

"Let's get out of here!" Cliff begged.

"With pleasure," replied Julian.

But before Julian could reactivate the shield, Cliff said, suddenly, "Wait!" Jumping off, he dashed back into the flames, finding now the wall of fire was much more difficult to negotiate.

Cliff was neither a scientist, nor a philosopher. He also did not quote rules and morals about doing things in the past to change history. But he was a cop, and he knew if left behind, the South could mass-produce the laser guns and possibly win the Civil War.

The smoke and heat had intensified. However, Cliff found the weapon and turned back toward the platform. His eyes were burning and he was completely surrounded by fire. He knew where he had to go but he had no idea how thick the fire was now.

Then he felt something strike his rear end. He whirled, drawing his sidearm. Surprisingly, he found no one there. Instead, he found six pieces of lit dynamite, tied together, at his feet. The fuse burned and hissed. He smelled the burning gunpowder. Cliff quickly spun around again. Yelling, he ran straight through the fire toward the Time Machine.

When he reached the other side he leapt onto the platform. Bill and Rusty began to smother his flames. "Dynamite! Dynamite!" Cliff said, pointing back into the fire from which he had just emerged. Julian wasted no time; he raised shields and pushed the manual override button. The very next thing he did was to don his glasses.

"Here put these on!" Bill demanded, hastily distributing glasses to everyone who was without, after pulling them out from a small compartment on the Time Machine. Everyone complied. Everything within the perimeter shimmered and began to phase out as time began to warp. All passengers except for Ricochet, who was unconscious, were able to see the inside of the barn as they were phasing out of the past. They saw a giant explosion from within as they were rocked, heavily.

The last thing Julian thought about before they began the time trip again was, "I hope that explosion doesn't throw our arrival time off for the future."

CHAPTER 5

"What happened? Cool, it must have all been a dream," Ricochet said. Moving his left arm, he felt pain in his upper chest and shoulder. "Well, I know at least this part wasn't a dream." He scrutinized the room he was in. Almost everything was white and there was a sterile smell to the place. In fact, he was the only thing of color in the room. There was quite a contrast between his deep-bronze skin color and the total whiteness of the room. He heard Lawrence Welk music playing in the background. "Dannng!" Ricochet said. "It's just my luck to die and go to the wrong Heaven. Now I have to listen to Lawrence Welk music the rest of my days."

In fact, he knew he was in a hospital room. He just didn't know which century. He noted the appearance of the room's decorations. Of course, he was back in the 21st century. His only concern at that time was where was everyone else. "Did they make it back alive?" he said.

At that moment Ham walked into his room. "Oh, it's about time you woke up, Sleepin' Booty," he said, jokingly. A guy gets shot in his bird chest and he thinks he can sleep for two days."

"What! I've been here for two days?" Ricochet asked, anxiously.

Ham smiled. "No, I was just kidding. You got here late last night. Rusty and Bill had taken Kat to the Underground Railroad. When they came back we were getting ready to fire up the Time Machine and come back. But a lynch mob surrounded us. Cliff held them off while we got the time machine started. We almost didn't make it. A bundle of dynamite exploded and the barn burned. But we made it, including Cliff. The first thing we had to do was get you to a hospital, so we brought you here. So, you see, you didn't miss anything exciting."

Taking a few seconds to absorb it all, Ricochet asked, "You mean Cliff risked his life just so we could get back to the future. Dannng. What about charges? Are they going to arrest us for breaking into the La Del building?"

"Nope. It's all taken care of. When we got back to the future we got back at almost the exact time we left. They never missed us. However, in order to keep this time travel thing a secret—even the government doesn't know about it—Julian and Bill's story was we were working with them in the building and they forgot to get clearance for us. Rusty and Cliff's police report indicates Rusty mistakenly shot you because he thought you were an intruder."

Sitting up in bed, Ricochet hung on to every word Ham spoke. When Ham finished, Ricochet reclined back on his bed. He sat still for a few seconds, as if frozen, and then spoke, "Dannng! I didn't know those scientists, and especially the cops, were that cool. They surprised the tar out of me."

Ham and Ricochet talked for a while longer. Most of Ricochet's questions were about Kat. He let his best friend know he really loved her. Doing his best to fill in the gaps for his friend, Ham assured him Kat was all right when they left her.

"Ham, I love her," Ricochet said.

Thinking Ricochet's professed love was merely infatuation, Ham sarcastically said, "Yeah, she looked real good. In fact, she looked like 'some Lord have mercy wrapped up in some save me Jesus'!" Laughing, he expected Ricochet to reciprocate in like fashion. Instead, he witnessed an unusually vulnerable heart from Ricochet.

"Stop playing! I'm serious. In the little time we spent together, I got to know her very well. And I love her very much. I must see her again."

Ham stared at Ricochet for a couple of seconds. "You're changing, man. I don't know what it was, whether it was Kat or maybe the time traveling scrambled your brain and heart. But you are different. You would have never fallen for a woman that fast, let alone, be this open about it. But I like it. This new found openness and vulnerability, you wear it well." Ham smiled, adding, "Maybe humility is next. I always thought you needed a little humility. Or was that humiliation? Well, either would do."

"Thanks. I think," replied Ricochet.

"Don't worry, 'Nothing is impossible with God,' so you may see Kat again." Ham reasoned.

Stunned, Ricochet asked, "Where'd you get that from? Are you going spiritual on me? Now you're changing." Ham smiled in response to the question. They continued to talk until Ricochet got tired. Actually, Ham got tired long before his friend, but he kept talking anyway.

Finally, Ricochet tired. He then turned his attention to his favorite pastime (other than baseball) – television. "I miss Kat, but I'm so glad to be back in the 21st century," Ricochet remarked, assuming a comfortable position, thinking of all the technological luxuries their time period offered. Even ten years ago most households, let alone, hospitals did not have such electronic niceties as wide-screen televisions. Ricochet scanned the channels to find something of interest to watch, finally stopping at a baseball game on the FOX Network. After watching for a few moments, he saw the teams were expansion teams. "These teams suck!" he remarked. "The only time either of them can win a game is when they play each other."

"Baseball is boring, why do you watch it?" Ham asked.

"No, just these two teams are boring, not baseball." Ricochet replied, "But I'll tell you what. If this batter doesn't get to first base, I'll change the channel." The count was no balls and two strikes. Painfully sitting up, Ricochet watched the game with a little more interest.

"Just a bit outside," the color commentator announced as the pitcher delivered ball two. Ricochet and Ham looked at each other and smiled. The pitch was actually more than just a bit outside. It missed the plate by almost two feet.

The color commentator was Bob Uecker, one of the most knowledgeable and comical announcers in the game. The next pitch was a fastball right down the middle of the plate. The batter jumped on it. With the loud crack of the bat, almost simultaneously, the pitcher's head snapped back, looking up and over his right shoulder. The left fielder raced toward the left field corner. The long fly ball hugged the foul line like a Koala bear climbing a tree. From the moment it had left the bat there was no doubt it would make it over the fence, deep in left field.

The question was, whether or not it would remain in fair territory. The left fielder reached the foul pole, looking up in time to see the ball, twenty feet over his head, curl just left of the pole before it passed it. The third base umpire signaled and yelled, "FOUL BALL."

The sigh of relief from the crowd and pitcher was so great the barometric pressure within the stadium increased. The home plate umpire tossed the pitcher a new ball. After setting up for the next pitch, he delivered it low and in the dirt for ball three. Making a trip to the back of the mound, the pitcher picked up the rosin bag, then angrily flung it down, raising a dust cloud behind the mound. He stepped on the rubber and received the sign from the catcher. The pitcher shook off three signs until he got the one he wanted. He delivered the pitch. It was a slow, hanging, curve ball that took forever to get to the plate.

Once the ball reached the plate, it broke ferociously down and away from the batter. The batter would probably estimate it broke about ninety degrees. However, it didn't matter because when he swung he was way out in front of the pitch, missing the ball completely. "Strike three," the home plate umpire yelled.

Coming out of his corkscrew-like swing, the batter took his bat, raised one knee, and broke it in two across his thigh. Some splinters flew away from the halved bat, while others lodged themselves, like needles, deep into the batter's thigh. Limping slightly, he headed back to the dugout. Bob Uecker remarked, "It's a good thing he's not the Grim Reaper. No one would ever die—not swinging like that."

After a long laugh, Ricochet kept his word and started scanning channels again. He finally stopped at CNN to watch a follow-up to a story that had unfolded a day ago. Awestruck, he stared at the screen in disbelief.

The story was about an American submarine attempting to rescue the crew of the Norwegian fishing vessel. However, as he watched the screen, the events of the story were very different than what he remembered. In the version he was now watching, all but three Norwegian crewmembers were rescued, and the captain of the *Finback* although injured, had survived.

In the version Ricochet remembered from the previous day, a lot of the Norwegian crew were not rescued and were presumed dead along with the captain of the *Finback*.

The most significant difference was the fact that the captain from the previous day's report was a White man named James English. The captain in the report in the hospital was an African-American named Fredward T. Hobbs.

Ricochet tried to explain the peculiar events to his friend, but the more he explained, the more he realized Ham was patronizing him. "I think you need some more rest," Ham said. Ricochet knew he had just traveled through time, been shot, and been unconscious for a long time. But he was sure those events had not made him delusional. Like anyone, he could be forgetful from time to time, but this wasn't a case of forgetfulness.

"I'm not crazy! I'll prove it to you. Where's my bag?" Ricochet inquired. Ham indicated it was in the car. After more than a little persuasion from Ricochet, Ham went to retrieve it.

Arriving back in the hospital room, he gave the duffel bag to Ricochet who searched frantically through it until he found an envelope containing a compact videodisc. Jumping out of bed, Ricochet installed it into the disc player built into the television. He searched through the disc, finally finding the spot he was looking for. He played it for Ham. It was just as Ricochet had said. They played it over and over, and each time, the captain of the *Finback* was white, and dead.

Neither Ham nor Ricochet knew exactly how, but they understood very well they had somehow disturbed the time line. The present had been altered. Ricochet eased into quietness. Ham knew Ricochet's next course of action would be well thought out. Reaching again into his duffel bag, Ricochet pulled out his laptop computer. Groaning because of his wound, he plugged it into the communication line jack in the hospital room. Once the computer was booted and a communication link established with the Ultra-Net, the cable began glowing a weak orange color. "Computer, give me National Birth Records," Ricochet commanded, speaking into the computer's installed microphone.

"Accessing," a computer-generated voice answered back.

Starting with Captain Hobbs of the *USS Finback*, Ricochet traced his genealogy back several generations until he found what he had already suspected. Captain Hobbs was a direct descendant of Kat, the woman whose life they had saved in the past. Talking about it, they realized Kat would have been killed by the slave catchers had it not been for the intervention of the time travelers. Also, the African-American captain of the *Finback*, Fredward Hobbs, would not even exist in their present timeline. Therefore, he wouldn't have been able to save anyone on the Norwegian fishing vessel.

Ricochet understood he was solely responsible for the way the events had unfolded. After all, it was he who, without thinking, had charged in to save Kat.

"But wait a minute. If we changed the future from the past, and the news report changed, then how come your disc didn't change? It has the same information it had on it before we left," Ham asked.

"I don't know, Ricochet replied, "Perhaps, because we had it with us in the past it was protected, as my memory of the events were protected. I am sure Julian and Bill can tell us." Terminating his connection to the Ultra-Net, Ricochet attempted to contact the two scientists.

"I'm sorry, Dr. Barnes, and Dr. Rousseau are unavailable at this time," responded the operator at La Del Technologies.

Ricochet slammed the telephone receiver down. "Man, forget all this calling stuff. What we need to do is go down there. I bet Rusty and Cliff could get us into that building."

"If they won't do it, I'll get us back in there" Ham reassured him. "Let's go down to the police station and get the boys with the badges."

"Wait a minute!" Ricochet said, lifting Ham's wrist to inspect his watch. "Dang! I was supposed to have picked up my nephew from my sister's house fifteen minutes ago. My sister and her husband are having marital problems, so they're going out of town. I promised to watch little Jerrick until his grandmother gets off work and picks him up. I'll tell you what, you go to the police station and get Rusty and Cliff. I'll meet you at La Del after I pick up Jerrick."

"How are you going to get out of the hospital?" Ham asked.

"Caveman power," Ricochet replied, I'm going to just use my feet and walk"

*****

Of course, Ricochet arrived at his sister's house late. Having not been officially discharged from the hospital, it took him longer to sneak out than he thought. And, of course, his sister and brother-in-law were upset. However, "What can they do about it?" Ricochet thought. He knew as soon as he got there, they would have to rush out of the door to catch their plane.

Little Jerrick sat in his high chair, doing almost everything except what he was supposed to be doing, eating his food. "Why didn't she feed him earlier? It's not like I didn't give her enough time," Ricochet complained. Leaning against the kitchen wall, he anxiously waited for Jerrick to finish. "Hurry up, little dude. We've got to jet!" Ricochet instructed. Then, he got an idea. "While I'm waiting on 'His Slowness, Jr.,' I can download more information from the Ultra Net," Ricochet said out loud.

He turned away from Jerrick and began downloading information, not knowing, mainly because he didn't have any kids, he had made a crucial error in the way he was feeding a two-year-old-child.

In less than a minute "His Slowness Jr." sensed he was no longer the focus of his uncle's attention. A short metallic tinkling sound suddenly mixed in with the working sound of the laptop computer's hard drive. Ricochet turned, bending down to pick up the source of the noise. "Here you are, little dude. Try to be more careful," Ricochet said after rinsing the spoon and handing it back to his nephew.

Ricochet then refocused on his computer. In less than a minute, he was disturbed again by the same tinkling sound. Once again, he rinsed and handed the spoon back to the toddler, saying, "As big as the table on this high chair is, I don't see how in the world you could drop anything on the floor." In a few more seconds, the spoon hit the floor again. Purposely, Ricochet didn't respond right away. Finally turning to Jerrick, saying sharply. "Come on kid, what do you have? Dropsy?" He rinsed the spoon and gave it back to Jerrick.

Hearing the nerve racking, tinkling noise upon the hard floor for the fourth and fifth times, Ricochet cringed, muttering something unrepeatable under his breath. However, after the sixth time it happened, he didn't even rinse the spoon. Handing it to his nephew, he said, "I hope you don't mind a little black grit." Confident this would not happen again, he resumed his work.

Then the unthinkable happened. Ricochet cringed again as he heard that metallic noise, that at first sounded so innocent, but now had matured into a nerve-wrecking sound. This time he turned around, saying, not in a low decibel voice, "That's all I can stands and I can't stands no more!" He picked up the spoon once again. Only this time Ricochet didn't give it directly to the child. Instead, he found the utility drawer in the kitchen and began rummaging through it. "Aha," he exclaimed, finding what he was looking for.

Taking the small cylindrical container, Ricochet removed the top. He squeezed a liberal amount on the handle of the spoon. Then he took the spoon and placed it in the eating hand of the youth. He compressed his nephew's hand around the slim metallic utensil for about three minutes. Letting go of the child's hand, he discovered his idea was working. The super glue held fast the spoon in Jerrick's hand. At first, little Jerrick was entertained; he tried to shake the spoon loose. Turning around, satisfied and proud, Ricochet resumed his work, without any further interruptions.

*****

Meanwhile, as it turned out, there was no need for Ham to put his skills to use again. Rusty and Cliff were very cooperative. They found the story quite intriguing, and definitely thought it was something Julian and Bill should know, if they didn't already.

"I don't care if they are unavailable or what your instructions are. Just get them. You tell them, the guys they hung out with last night are here to see them, and one of them is a real ticked-off cop." The receptionist cut off the intercom that transmitted the voice from one side of the security glass to the other. Rolling her eyes and turning her back, she made a call on the inter-building com-phone. She lowered her voice so they could not hear her, however, she could only lower her voice so low before the person on the other end of the call couldn't hear her either.

Through the vents in the thick glass barrier, Rusty could still make out some of her verbiage. A half smile developed on his face as he heard her repeat, "ticked-off cop" to the person on the other end. Returning to the security glass, she informed the visitors a security guard would be there in forty-five seconds to escort them back to Dr. Barnes' office.

"Why couldn't she just say a minute instead of forty-five seconds?" Rusty thought. Engineers and scientists were just too exact for him. He never felt comfortable around them.

At that time, Ricochet walked up, joining his friends. He carried Jerrick in his arms. No one said anything about it, but they did wonder, including the receptionist, why the child was carrying a spoon. "He's with us," Rusty remarked to the receptionist.

The security guard escorted the visitors to Dr. Barnes' office. Still in some obvious pain, Ricochet eyed the security guard very closely. He was almost sure this guard was one of the guards who had taken a shot at him the night before. As soon as the guard excused himself, it was like a reunion. All six men who had just made history were once again united.

Ricochet, Rusty, Cliff and Ham, all started talking at once. "Hold up! Just one person tell me what's going on," Julian interrupted.

Ricochet spoke first. He explained the whole situation about Kat and the captain of the *Finback* to Julian and Bill. They listened intently. Then Ricochet played the disc.

There was no doubt in Julian's mind. It was exactly as Ricochet presumed. History had indeed been altered and all the men in that room were responsible for it. Was there anything they could do about it, Julian asked himself? His brain was throbbing. Not being able to come up with any solutions, Julian suggested they adjourn. He needed time to collect his thoughts.

"It's not everyday you travel over a hundred and fifty years into the past, almost getting killed by people who died long before you were born," he said. "Let me have all of your numbers and I will give you a call in a few days.
Remember this is top-top secret." Now the six men were a team— The Time Team.

But before leaving, Ricochet pulled Julian aside, asking, "Do you have any glue solvent?"

CHAPTER 6

Using his right hand, Julian clasped his unlined leather jacket in a feeble attempt to form a thermal barrier between his exposed neck and the environment. It had been just over 24 hours since his unscheduled trip to the 19th century. The mercury had plummeted 30 degrees since then. Due to lack of sleep, the bulkiness of his briefcase and the awkwardness of the files he was attempting to carry, Julian made another feeble attempt. This time it was in trying to close the car door. It took him a total of three attempts, including two attempts made with his rear end before he could successfully close the door. Then he focused on retrieving the fallen files.

Though it had been a while since he had seen his wife, he had managed to call her. He told her there was an emergency at the laboratory and he would be there all night. But, he had neglected to tell her he would not be home until late the next evening.

Julian had set the Time Machine so they would return at precisely the same moment in the present they had left. But, by the time the Time Team had taken Ricochet to the hospital and covered up any evidence of them ever leaving on the Time Machine, it was already way into the wee hours of the morning. It made sense to stay at the La Del Laboratory over night. Fortunately, he had a change of clothes and a shower stall in his laboratory.

When Julian walked through his front door he felt as tired as Ralph Cramden from The Honeymooner's television show coming home from a hard day's work on the bus. The events of the last 24 hours had given him a pounding stress headache that was screaming out for medication. Desperately, he wanted to take a couple of Tylenol Fives and go directly to bed. He knew he had the problems with the time travel events to work out. However, that would have to wait because Jasmine would most definitely want to fight.

He couldn't much blame her; after all, he wasn't the world's greatest husband. Often taking her for granted and not spending much time with her, Julian was always putting his work first.

He hoped his wife would be asleep, as he had not heard her since he got into the house. Normally, she'd wake up when the computer announced him. Going into the kitchen to get the Tylenol Fives out of the cabinet, Julian noticed a note on the microwave, which read, "Dinner is in the microwave and wine is on the table. Love Jasmine."

"Good, she must have gone out," he thought. Julian noticed there was a lot of food, but he was too tired and stressed to eat. With heavy steps, he climbed the stairs toward the bedroom. Stopping momentarily at the end of the first flight, gazing at their wedding photographs. He envied the happiness and love in the pictures, wondering what happened to them.

When he entered the bedroom, he found Jasmine sitting up in bed, wearing very sexy, peach-colored nightwear, his favorite. There was a bottle of wine and two glasses on the nightstand.

Julian glanced at his wife. But, it was her seductive and suggestive bedroom eyes that followed his every move around the room. Her glass, stained with red lipstick, was half full. But judging from the amount of wine missing from the bottle, she had consumed a lot more than half a glass. Partly because he was extremely tired, but more because he had just gotten used to it over the last couple of months, Julian looked at her, saying, "I'm tired; I'm not in the mood." Jasmine's face dropped. The sum of all the hurt from the past months overtook her heart like a 150-knot hurricane.

Without so much as a clue he had deeply hurt his wife, Julian undressed and got into the shower. Jasmine sat there with many questions running through her head. Was her husband gay? Was he having an affair? Does he love me anymore? She could have accepted "yes" to one or both of the first two questions quite more easily than to the third.

Jasmine was a very attractive woman. Her athletic, slim, and tall build often attracted more attention than she preferred, especially when she worked out at the health spa. She and Julian had met in college. Though her beauty would definitely get a man's attention from across the room, Julian had married her for her intelligence and independence also. After college, she went to law school and became a very powerful attorney. But after a few years she became despondent with the politics and the dishonesty in that profession. She opened a large child development center for children, with locations in Detroit and Lawrenceville, Georgia, calling them "Jesus and Me Leaning Centers," so she could teach Christian values to children.

Jasmine's problem was after all the years of neglect and being taken for granted she was still in love with her workaholic husband.

One day she hoped they could have children. But, they would never have any children if her husband wouldn't make love to her. At this point in their marriage, Julian would rather save the world than make love to his wife. Jasmine would never dream of interfering with his work. But she was puzzled as to why he couldn't do both.

She reached toward the nightstand. Instead of picking up her glass, Jasmine jerkily picked up the bottle. Turning it up in a single motion, she brought it quickly to her lips, lacking a noticeable amount of dexterity. She did, however, manage to safely stop the forward motion of the bottle before she cracked a tooth. When she tilted her head back, the condensation that had formed near the bottom of the bottle mimicked the tears that ran from her eyes to her ears.

The cold, tiny water drops, which mimicked the green color of the wine bottle, ran a jagged track along the neck of the bottle. Their final destination was her lips, which by then were nearly depleted of lipstick. Although the distance the condensation had to travel was longer than the distance from her eyes to her ears, she managed to hold the bottle up long enough for the water drops to reach her lips.

Not many women would have stood for the lack of love in her marriage she had endured over the last three months. It would have been totally different if she were physically separated from her husband because of work. But to be separated mentally, emotionally, and physically was completely unacceptable, especially while they still lived in the same house, sleeping in the same bed almost every night.

Jasmine slipped under the covers, weeping silently upon her pillow. At first, she had wept out loud for ten seconds. Then, reminding herself she was a strong Black woman, she changed her weeping to a heart-wrenching but silent cry, which escalated the hurt even more.

Jasmine was unaware of the passage of time, but fifteen minutes had passed since she laid her head on her pillow. The pillow was slightly wet from her tears and stained from the makeup and tear mixture. Yet, it still hinted of her sweet perfume.

Hearing Julian finish in the shower, she wiped her face, quickly. Julian exited the shower, totally oblivious to Jasmine's earlier crying. But, by intermittent rustling sounds he could tell she was still awake. He climbed into the bed. Getting comfortable, he let out a big sigh. Then, turning his back to her and pulling the covers with him, Julian said, "Goodnight, Honey."

Not giving up so easily, Jasmine tried the physical approach. She started massaging Julian's neck and back. He didn't object to it; it was relieving a lot of tension in his neck. As a matter of fact, he welcomed it with a sigh of enjoyment and a low moan.

Julian was a tight muscular man, but Jasmine knew her husband well. She could tell most of the extra tightness she felt in his upper body was due to stress. After massaging his neck and back for a few minutes she wanted to give her fingers a rest, so she tried a different tactic. Julian flinched slightly when his wife started kissing his neck softly. It wasn't a flinch of disdain, more surprise. However, Jasmine mistook it for the former.

Subsequently, Julian's stomach growled, loudly. "Are you hungry, Baby?" asked Jasmine. "Didn't you see the food in the microwave?"

Normally, Julian would have taken time to think about his answer, but he was much too tired. Answering her truthfully, but with little regard for her feelings, he uttered, "I saw it. But I didn't feel like eating. I didn't know how long it had been out, so I threw it in the trash."

As soon as the words had left his mouth he knew he had said the wrong thing. At first, he thought maybe he would get away with it, since Jasmine started to talk about something else. She stammered on a word, then, cutting her sentence off in midstream, responded. " . . . you threw it away?" Jasmine demanded, compressing her anger. Her voice was now a little higher in pitch and amplitude.

"You mean I've been up waiting for you to come home. I get off work and cook for you, save your food, and you won't even show me enough gratitude to say thank you or at least eat one morsel. We won't even mention the fact that you haven't made love to me in months!" Her fingers had been massaging Julian's shoulders and back, at the base of his neck. Then they went motionless. As her voice increased in amplitude, the fingernails began, ever so slowly, to dig into his skin.

"I'm tired of this stuff! All I do is try to love you. And you can't love me back. This has been going on for three months now. Maybe it wouldn't be so bad if you would at least have sex with me every now and then. At this point I wouldn't even care if you read the newspaper while I had sex with you! What is it? Do you and Bill have something going on?"

It was as if someone had opened the flood gates, or more like, there was a catastrophic failure of the dike since there was no control at all of her fury. Until this point, she had played the supportive Christian housewife. She thought Julian was being overworked, so she wanted to stand by his side.

"Stand by his side. Stand by his side." She said, bobbing her head up and down, and from side to side, mocking the psychologist and Christian advisor that had given her that advice. Now, she didn't care about much except to vent three months of bottled up feelings.

Julian was tired but he wasn't stupid. He listened to her without saying a word, but he struggled to not fall asleep on her. Then the pressure from her fingernails, increased to intense pain.

"Hey!" he yelled, leaping out of bed and spinning to face her. Jasmine fell on her side but quickly recovered and perched herself upon the bed. He rubbed the spot on his neck that had felt good just moments before. Examining his fingertips, Julian found blood. "What in the world is wrong with you, Woman?" is what Julian intended to say, but all he got out was, "What in the world is wrong with you, Wo . . . ," before Jasmine lunged toward him like she had been shot out of a cannon.

Julian saw her flying toward him with eyes that burned. She became a human missile. Suddenly she was all over him, beating him about the head. Julian managed to block most of the blows but occasionally the underside of a stray fist would find its mark. He tried to grab both her wrists but they were moving much too fast. Trying another method, he sidestepped to his right, then quickly to the left, and then back to the right again. Jasmine shadowed his first and second movements but was unable to counteract his third move. She was caught completely off guard by one of his old basketball moves. Julian had learned it from an old friend. Erin Moody was his name and he was an Army boxer. Julian had lost track of Moody years ago. But he now made a mental note to thank him if he ever saw him again.

This gap in her reflexes allowed Julian to spin behind her back and grab her around the shoulders with both arms. Then he lowered his grasp, so as he could wrap her entire torso, including her arms, with his arms. Julian had now succeeded in completely immobilizing his wife. Or so he thought.

Being trapped was not a feeling Jasmine was all too fond of. She went completely wild, screaming, struggling and kicking at her husband. Julian did well to move his legs out of the way of each back kick while still holding on. It was almost akin to holding a wild mustang.

Jasmine allowed her body to suddenly go totally limp. Although she did not weigh much, she almost literally poured right out of her husband's grasp. In order to compensate, Julian tightened his grip and fell to the floor along with Jasmine. They lay on the floor together. Jasmine's back was toward Julian, while he still kept her in a tight embrace.

Realizing her attempt to liberate herself from Julian's grip was ineffective, she once again became violent. This time, besides screaming, struggling, and kicking, she tried to roll out of his grip.

Julian held Jasmine firmly in his arms while they rolled around on the floor, in one direction then another, knocking nightstands over and bumping into other bedroom furniture. Convinced there was no way she could escape his grasp, he decided to have a little fun with her. His arms were wrapped around her body, tightly; both laid on their right sides panting heavily. Her back was pulled tightly against Julian's chest making it quite easy for him to put his lips close to her left ear and whisper, "You know the best thing I like about you right now?"

Jasmine stopped struggling as Julian paused for effect and just in case she wanted to answer. When only silence filled the air, he knew two things. The first was he had her attention. The second was she was not in the mood to answer. So he answered, "My arms. That's what I like best about you right now," Julian chuckled.

Jasmine was not slow mentally by any stretch of the imagination, especially when it came to understanding jokes. But this time, it took a full two seconds for it to register in her head the man she loved, whom she was fighting, was laughing at her. And once she realized it, she responded instantly. And once again, Julian wished he had not said something.

Suddenly, like a hornet's nest that has been stirred up, Jasmine's savage metamorphosis was quick, painful and relentless. She still couldn't break Julian's grip, but he suffered dearly from it. Kicking him repeatedly with piston-like back kicks, she caused Julian a constellation of stars of pain. Yet, he tightened his grip. If she could cause that much pain to him while he had her under control, she would probably kill him if she were free.

She kept kicking him until her legs grew tired. Then she managed to roll herself and Julian over at least five to ten more times. Not counting, Julian focused on trying to anticipate her next move.

Jasmine had started out strong when they first fell to the floor. Now, more than fifteen minutes had passed and she was showing signs of fading. The frequency and strength of her outbursts were slowly diminishing, while her breathing was getting much heavier. Julian was also getting tired. However, he found he could still hold her while reducing most of the pressure he was exerting on her. He would reduce it while she was in a rest cycle and reapply it as soon as she started to struggle again. It was during one of the struggles he bumped his head on one of the legs of the bed. It was all he could do to keep from releasing his grasp to rub his head to check if she had drawn blood again.

After about twenty more minutes of this, she lay there breathing hard, still embraced by Julian. Yet it wasn't an embrace of passion, it was more an embrace of protection, as far as Julian was concerned. Finally, the exertion and exhaustion had completely drained her of strength and will. She lay there in Julian's grasp. Her panting began to subside.

They lay on their sides, upon the bedroom floor, motionless and silent. Jasmine's back was toward Julian and he maintained the clutch in case after her rest she wanted to continue to struggle. Then another five minutes passed and his wife still remained motionless. He thought she must be asleep or extremely tired.

Julian raised his head so he would be able to look at the side of her face. He could tell she was still awake but to his surprise, she was silently crying. Then he was reminded of something he already knew; she was indeed beautiful. This was the first time something like this ever happened to them and he knew it was totally his fault. Looking at his wife again, Julian thought of their lives they had spent together since they had first met.

Impulsively, Julian kissed the side of his wife's neck. He slowly and carefully moved his left hand downward until it rested on top of Jasmine's left hand. He lightly caressed her everywhere his hand made contact with her body along the way. Jasmine remained almost perfectly still, only exhibiting occasional sensations as a result of the light intermittent contact from Julian's hand.

At this point, Julian realized he had been a total jerk for the last three months. He also knew, no response from his wife right now was a good response. Jasmine had been trying to make their marriage better. Now, Julian realized he had been the cause of all the problems. Until now, in fact, he hadn't realized there was a real problem. He hoped he could only be so lucky if she had not cheated on him.

Julian allowed her enough room to roll over and turn around. He turned her around so she faced him. Jasmine offered no resistance. There was a scary duality about her; she was completely submissive. Julian took his hand and raised her head so she would be looking directly into his face. Their eyes met for the first time that entire evening. Looking at his beautiful wife, Julian's heart dropped, as now he saw the full evidence that she had been silently crying. All the time she had her back to him, lying quietly, a steady flow of tears had fallen from her eyes onto her cheeks and then onto the carpet. It was much like rain as it dripped though the ceiling of a leaky roof onto a carpet. Only her tears were much quieter. Still totally drained, Jasmine spoke no words. Julian uttered only a few. Through his tears, he said, "I'm sorry, Baby. I'm sorry for everything. I love you very much."

Crying together, they made love. That night, Julian made love to his wife like he had never done before. He also realized somewhere along the way he had stopped loving her as his wife, not just physically. Emotionally, he had put her through a lot over the last three months. The fact that she stuck by him was a testimony of her love for him. That night Julian's repentance would serve as a testimony for her and God.

After making love, they talked the rest of the night. The alarm clock sounded at its normal time, 5:15 a.m.; they were still talking. Julian and Jasmine had bared their bodies, their hearts, their souls and their love to each other during the night and through the early morning. He finally told her all about his work, including the time travel when they met Kat.

Jasmine, in turn, told Julian about how close she had been to having an affair, but she had changed her mind because she loved him very much and she didn't want to break the vows she had made to God. They cried in each other's arms several more times during the early morning. They tasted each other's salty kisses as they embraced and cried together. But when the alarm clock sounded, Julian and Jasmine stopped talking. They lay there embracing each other so tightly, that, like the scenes of lovers Julian saw while time traveling, only their closeness concealed them. They then made love again and again.

It was a beautiful sunny mid-morning as Julian and Jasmine arose. They were still tired, but neither of them were normally late sleepers, so they got up. Julian and Jasmine spent the majority of the day like newlyweds: taking turns feeding and caressing each other. Julian knew in his heart he was very lucky not to have lost his wife after totally neglecting and ignoring her over the last three months. He thanked God continuously, as he and his wife got down on their knees and prayed to the Father in the middle of the night. They decided they would start going to church together, something Jasmine had always wanted them to do. As a scientist, Julian had found it hard to believe in God. Two totally different events from the last two evenings, however, convinced him he might have been wrong in that area. His friend Bill, who was a disciple of Christ, had tried to persuade Julian to come to church over the last four years. Blowing him off, Julian would say something like, "I don't believe in God, and He doesn't believe in me."

The sun was now diminishing from a bright-yellow color to a mellower shade of orange as it started on its daily retirement ritual. The sunlight, accompanied by its welcomed warmth, shined into the west-end windows of Julian and Jasmine's home. Although it would disappear over the horizon in an hour, the arm-like rays of the sun never seemed to understand this event. This was demonstrated as the rays shown through the window. It was as if a hand with long fingers attached to the end of each ray tried desperately to grab hold of any piece of furniture or window sill, trying to prevent the sun from disappearing each night. Then in time, like it always happened the solar hands would lose their grips, allowing the day to reluctantly but willingly give way to the night.

The den was at the west-end of the house. There, Julian and Jasmine sat in a comfortable leather chair. With the chair wrapped around him and his arms wrapped around his wife, who sat in front of him, they watched television. They had been there for an hour, laughing, talking and caressing each other. There was a short announcement saluting the achievements of the late Dr. Martin Luther King, Jr. coming from the television. Suddenly, Jasmine turned back around, facing the television. Julian looked up.

These "Moments in History" public service announcements had been running on the different stations, off and on for the last few days. This one began with the audio portion of the beginning of Dr. King's "I Have a Dream" speech.

Then the television displayed scenes from the march on Washington D.C., the Montgomery Bus Boycott, and also scenes from the 1963 march in Birmingham, Alabama. The Birmingham March had the most horrific scenes. This was the march where Bull Connors, the city's Commissioner of Public Safety, ordered the fire engines to turn the high-pressured water hoses on the young marchers, flattening most of them against the sidewalk. He also ordered the police dogs let loose on the marchers. Who would not be moved by the colored youth captured on film, being beat down, relentlessly, by a police officer with his nightstick, while simultaneously being mauled by a police dog?

As she watched, Jasmine sighed, saying, "If Dr. King were alive today, the world would be so different." Julian wasn't really listening to her, but instead listening to the television. However, he heard enough of it for it to catch his attention.

"What did you say?" he asked.

She repeated it to him, and then asked, "Why?" She heard only dead silence, not even a rustle from movement. Jasmine turned again to look at her husband. She saw a far-away look in his eyes that was all too familiar. She knew he was formulating a plan. Then, she understood. "No, no Julian, no!" she screamed, suddenly.

CHAPTER 7

"Excuse me," Ham said.

"Pardon me," added Ricochet as they stepped over the feet of everyone, seeking two empty seats.

"Well, I'm glad everyone is here. Now we can begin," Julian announced. Julian, Bill, Cliff and Rusty had been waiting patiently for Ham and Ricochet to arrive.

Almost a week had passed since their unexpected excursion into the nineteenth century. Julian had telephoned each of them the evening before, asking them to meet with him. He told all of them the meeting was of paramount importance. And all, including Bill, were in the dark as to the reason for the meeting. Julian had confided only in Jasmine. After he got everyone's full attention, he started.

"Gentlemen, I'm glad all of you could make it this evening, though some of you are on *Colored People* time." He smiled, looking at Ham and Ricochet. "What I'm about to propose to you will require all of our cooperation. We will need to be in unity, much like we were when we time traveled last week

"All of us are aware of how our last trip resulted in us unintentionally altering the time line, thus altering the future. If you remember, I was one of the biggest opponents against interfering with the natural course of events in the past. I knew it could eventually affect the future, even as far as actually terminating our own existence. We still don't know, and will never know how far-reaching the repercussions will be because of our tampering with time. Suppose one of Kat's descendants kills one of you guys. Or, what if one of the slave catcher's descendants was destined to be an Adolph Hitler. If that were the case, we would have done the world a great favor."

Ricochet leaned back in his chair, cradling his chin with the "L" formed by his index finger and thumb. Ham sat forward on the edge of his chair. Bill had never sat down, but he had stopped pacing. Rusty and Cliff, in typical law enforcement fashion, sat with their backs against the wall closest to the exit.

"I know you are all probably wondering where I'm going with this. My wife, Jasmine, has given me an excellent idea. It goes against everything I believe. However, like Burger King used to say, 'Sometimes you just gotta break the rules,'" Julian exclaimed, displaying a half smile. "Technically, we're really not breaking the rules. We're in unexplored territory; we're making up the rules as we go along."

"Gentlemen, this is what I propose. We all know Dr. Martin Luther King's birthday is the 15th of January. I would love for all of us to see him at his 79th birthday party. 'How?' you may ask." Julian paused for effect.

"We will go on a mission to the past, and save Dr. King's life." Julian paused again.

The room was completely quiet. In fact, it was so quiet that one could hear a mouse urinating on a cotton ball. But before Julian could continue Ricochet spoke up. "You mean, prevent his assassination?"

"That's exactly what I mean!" answered Julian.

"Cool. I like it. Imagine what the world would be like if he were alive today," said Ricochet.

"Well, suppose we did save him? That doesn't mean he would be alive today. He could die of natural causes, or some other redneck could kill him."

"That's right. We don't know, but I think it's worth the effort to find out. Don't you?" Julian offered.

Hesitating, as if he didn't really want to share what he said next, Julian looked up and confessed, "You know, I want you all to know something. This is not a whim. I've wrestled with the ethical implications of doing this. I've been thinking about this every since we came back from the 1800's. I've even devised entire plans of how we can go about it."

Julian drew in a deep breath and exhaled slowly before continuing. "I told you my wife gave me this idea. She didn't do it intentionally. You see, my marriage was already in trouble and when I told Jasmine what I wanted to do, she hit the ceiling. We fought for several days. I first thought it was luck she didn't leave me, but thanks to her I know why. It was because of God. During those couple of days, we learned a lot about each other's beliefs. When all was said and done, she finally understood my deep conviction for this mission and conceded, but only with concessions from me, also. After we prevent King's assassination, I will reluctantly quit my job. But, the up side to that is I will get to spend more time with her. "The most important concession that I made was to go to church with my wife and study the Bible until I'm ready to get baptized."

The others had been sitting silently, listening to Julian. When he had paused, no one said anything until Ricochet broke the silence again. "Amen brotha! That's exactly where you need to have your heathen, nutty-professor butt, in church." There were a few chuckles around the room but none were from Bill. Julian noticed, making a mental note.

Julian continued. "Truth be known, I think I'm getting the best parts of the deal. First, we get to save Dr. King's life. Then I get to spend more time with my wife, and more importantly with my God. Frankly gentlemen, I want and need all the help on this I can get. My mind is made up. I'm going to do this. The only question is, are *we* going to do this together as the Time Team, or am I going to do this alone? Feedback gentlemen?"

At once, most everyone spoke up. They asked many questions about how they would accomplish the task of saving Dr. King. They wanted to be a part of it.

There was, however, one voice physically standing alone. It was Bill's. He was the last person Julian expected would have a problem with this idea. Julian thought it would have been Rusty, if it were anyone. Bill argued it wasn't the most ethical thing to do. "I understand exactly how *you* people feel, but we shouldn't tamper with history."

As soon as it was uttered, Julian could feel the tension in the room escalate. Ham immediately became very defensive, verbally assaulting Bill. It wasn't everything Bill had said that pushed Ham into such a fury. It was just two words, "you people." These two words had been a sore spot with African-Americans ever since Ross Perot uttered them when he addressed African-Americans during a speech, almost twenty years prior, during his presidential campaign in the early 1990s. A confrontation was the last thing Julian wanted.

Julian had said earlier in the meeting he would accomplish it without anyone's help if he had to, even though it wouldn't be easy. Studying the plans over and over since he had conceived them, he knew it was going to take the help and cooperation of everyone in that room to accomplish this in the most efficient manner. By "efficient manner," Julian meant no other lives would be lost. Not just their lives but also any lives from any century, as had been the result of their messy first time travel.

Interrupting the argument between Bill and Ham, Julian said, "People, people!" As abruptly as it had started, the argument ended. "People," he continued, "Would you all agree to at least let me show you the plans for this mission before you make up your minds?" Everyone, except Bill said yes. But after a little prodding from Julian, he finally agreed to take a look.

Julian produced maps, articles, plans, videodiscs, and all the other training aids he had put together. It was as if they were in school. Before they started, Julian turned toward Rusty, Cliff, Ricochet and Ham, saying, "You guys are the professionals, I'm going to need a lot of help from you. As you can see no one gets hurt and minimum lives are changed significantly," Julian said, concluding his explanation of the mission. "Any questions?" he added.

Rusty suggested they change some steps of the plan because Julian had assumed police response times were longer in the 1960s. Rusty pointed out the response times may have seemed longer but in actuality it was the communication time that was longer. Julian agreed. Then Ham suggested how they should take out the assassin, altering Julian's plan slightly. In a few minutes all of the former time travelers, including Bill, were participating. For the next four hours they perfected the plans. Inwardly, Julian patted himself on the back for a job well done. Although, he would probably never admit it to anyone, he had secretly planned to unite the Time Team by purposely engineering his plans with hidden flaws. Thus, trained eyes could spot the flaws and everyone would participate.

However, when Julian inquired again that evening, everyone, but Bill wanted to be part of this mission. Bill had softened up considerably, but he still had reservations. He told Julian he needed time to think.

*****

It had been one week since Julian had disclosed his intention and plans to stop the assassination of Dr. King to his partners. They had all been practicing and fine-tuning the mission during that time. Though Bill had not yet informed Julian of his intent to participate in the actual mission, he worked on several practice runs. Julian and the others had also practiced a set of contingency plans just in case Bill decided against participating.

It was the evening before the Time Team was to embark upon its mission. They had just finished a last walk-through, a scenario in which Bill did not participate. Originally, the last walk-through was supposed to include Bill. However, Bill was late--very late--so Julian decided to rehearse Plan B, which did not include Bill.

Completing the test run, Julian, Ricochet, Rusty, Ham and Cliff congratulated each other. They had originally bonded because of their initial experience together during the accidental time travel to the nineteenth century. However, because of his several missed sessions and his noncommittal attitude, Bill had become an outcast. Arriving at the Barnes' household at 10:15 p.m., Bill rang the doorbell. This was very different from his normal routine of just entering. Jasmine opened the door and was very pleased to see him. They hugged. They had hugged before on many occasions, but somehow this was a little different. Jasmine could tell he was tenser than usual.

"What's wrong?" she asked. Looking straight into her eyes, Bill explained to her how he felt about the mission. His speech was full of prattle, and he looked toward the ground as he spoke. Jasmine hugged him again and told him, "Jules is in the study."

Entering Julian's study, Bill found a rushed silence as all eyes fell upon him. Walking immediately up to Julian, Bill said, sheepishly, "Can I talk to you for a minute?"

They walked outside of the room, by the door, talking in hushed voices. Placing his ear against the door, Ricochet tried to listen. He couldn't make out much, but at one point he thought he heard Julian say, "You're crazy." Then there was silence.

The next thing Ricochet heard and felt was a loud thud. The door opened quickly and without warning, hitting him in his ear and head. Re-entering the room with a very solemn look on his face, Julian gave Ricochet a sideways glance as he walked by him. Ricochet noticed neither the glance nor the solemn look. He was too busy holding his ear.

Looking at all of them except Ricochet, who was standing beside him, Julian announced, "We leave tonight without him." He then informed everyone Bill thought they were playing God. Not only was he not going to be a part of it, he also couldn't stand idly by and let them do it. He planned to go to the authorities. Julian, determined to not let anything stop him, told Bill they would delay the mission one day so everyone could talk it over and vote on it. Actually, Julian was attempting to buy them some time. They would need as much as they could get.

Dismissing the rest of the team, Julian told them he would see them in a few hours.

*****

At 1:00 a.m., the Time Team arrived in the laboratory. They had been awake all day practicing the mission. Ready and trained, they were, only extremely fatigued. They had planned to get adequate rest before their journey began, but circumstances had changed and prevented that.

Julian collected the old mission plans and handed out new ones. The new plans were a secret contingency plan he had developed once he knew Bill opposed the mission. No one knew about these plans except Jasmine.

With haste, Julian performed the pre-checks before getting underway. He assigned everyone something to do. The checklist was completed faster than usual. After loading all their equipment onto the platform, Julian made the weight adjustments. There was much more equipment to load now than on their initial accidental time travel.

Although they didn't have a lot of time to go over the new mission plans, Julian had the utmost confidence in these men. He had tried to plan for every possibility, knowing something unplanned would more than likely happen during the mission. Everyone boarded the time platform. Then Julian initiated the countdown sequence. Time began to count down just as before.

When ten seconds remained the shield would automatically energize as before, but this time Julian manually activated the shields at twenty seconds. Call it a gut feeling; call it intuition; or, call it luck. Whatever it was called, Julian was just glad he called it.

Suddenly, the laboratory doors burst open. In rushed Bill, accompanied by ten FBI agents with guns drawn.

"Stop! Dr. Julian Barnes. By order of the United States government, I order you to shut this time machine down!" barked the FBI agent in charge.

"Ten seconds left to time travel, seven, six . . . ," the computer announced. Checking the computer controls, Bill reluctantly informed the head agent Julian had overridden the manual shutdown, thus the time machine could not be stopped.

"Four, three . . . ," the computer generated voice continued.

Without many options left, the head FBI agent fired his gun at the Time Machine; his droned agents followed suit. Before fading out of the 21st century, Julian saw Bill immediately hit the deck when the FBI agents started firing. Sparks jumped off the rose-colored shield as each bullet struck it. One of the agents fell to the ground awkwardly, a victim of stray bullets that had ricocheted off the shield.

*****

Inhaling, Julian concluded that alleys thirty years in the past were just as acrid as they were in the 21st century. Thirty years didn't seem to make much of a difference. He hadn't been in as many alleys as some of the other men who accompanied him on the mission, but he'd been in enough. They all smelled like rotted garbage and baked urine.

The members of the Time Team had been looking around since they materialized in an alley that was located in a run-down district of abandoned warehouses. It was almost dusk. There was very little light from the semi-functioning streetlights. However, it didn't take very much light to see the garbage, which was a major source of the stench, piled very high in that alleyway. It was also a warm evening, which helped little in stifling the stench.

Rusty and Cliff scrutinized the situation very differently from the other team members. They took defensive stances with weapons drawn, as if entering a hostile situation. After the events of their last time travel, they were taking no chances. Ricochet inhaled and said, "So, this is what Memphis smelled like thirty years ago."

Julian replied, "If this is Memphis on April 2, 1968, the garbage men are on strike."

Rusty and Julian began to confer. After a few seconds, Rusty sent Cliff on a reconnaissance mission, saying, "Find out where we are in Memphis, and a good place to stash the Time Machine and our gear."

Ham, Rusty, Ricochet and Julian began to break down the Time Machine so it would be easy to transport. Although it was heavy, it had retractable wheels that made it easy to transport. While they were involved with that task, Rusty, who had been focusing his attention elsewhere, said, "Maybe I should have gone with him, this being the 1960s, and all. There are a lot of racists out there."

Ham responded abruptly, "Man, this ain't the wild-wild-west, and it most definitely ain't slave times. This is the 1960s. The time of Marvin Gaye—'What's Going On,' and James Brown—'Jump back, wanna kiss myself.'" He ended that sentence by doing a James Brown dance step. Then he collapsed to the ground upon one knee with his head down, waiting for someone to drape an imaginary cape over him.

Of course, Ricochet obliged him. Ham rose, threw off the make-believe cape and looked directly at Rusty, responding, "He'll be I-ight."

Ricochet interjected, "Besides, when it comes to racism in the 60s, history speaks mostly of the bad deeds done by white people. There were actually a lot of good white people in the 1960s. So, I don't think we have to worry about too many white people harming Cliff."

Rusty, who had been looking down while working with the Time Platform, looked up at Ricochet, saying with a smile, "I was talking about protection from the Black people."

The warmth of Rusty's smile invited warmth in return, not confrontation. As it was, all the men laughed together.
Ricochet looked at Ham, saying, "Oh, he got jokes."

Suddenly, a rustling noise came from a dimly lit portion of the alley. Drawing their guns, the team members wheeled about. "Who's there?" Julian shouted. There was no answer but the noise continued. It became more frantic. "I said, 'Who's there'? If you don't come out in the open, we're going to open fire in five seconds," Julian called.

A frail, harsh-looking man, who seemed to be searching for his bearings, emerged from under a pile of garbage. His plaid clothes were badly soiled and ragged. He complained bitterly, struggling to stand erect. "Can't a man sleep in peace and private in his own home? Lousy, good-for-nothing hippies." The man had a scraggly, tangled beard and the few teeth in his mouth were black with decay. The varicose veins in his abnormally large nose looked like rivers. He was a White man, but due to the layers of dirt on his face and hands, it was difficult to tell.

He finally stumbled to his feet, and made his way toward Ricochet. He stumbled and Ricochet caught him. Holding him, Ricochet thought, "He might not be the only stinky thing in this alley, but he sure is a major contributing factor." "What year is it, old man?" Ricochet asked, as he stood him up.

When the old man spoke, the debris from his mouth became missiles, launched in the general direction of Ricochet. Ricochet tensed. But like a Scud, the debris never found its mark, falling harmlessly to the ground. "It's 1492 and you just discovered America. Congratulations, Christopher Columbus!" the bum said, sarcastically, smiling as he saluted Ricochet. "Or should I say Coal-lumbus, colored boy?" He continued to taunt Ricochet. "Whatsa matter? You have too much pot? I told you that stuff was bad for your memory."

He made a sweeping gesture, including all the men in the alley. "I told ya! I told ya all! I said that pot was no good for you. But no, you just wanted to smoke your hippie lungs away and have orgies and chant 'bout free love. Now look at ya. Just look at ya now!" Settling down somewhat, the old bum looked the Time Team over again. Then, he lowered his head in disgust and shook it from side to side, saying, "Pit-a-ful."

"Sir," Julian pleaded, "All we want to do is ask you some real quick questions. Then you can go."

"Can go?" snapped the old bum. "This is my home! Y'ain't making me go nowhere. Yaw going to be the ones that go. In fact, yaw can get out of here right now. So, get to steppin'." Facing Ricochet, the old bum pointed toward the end of the alley as if it were the front door. He had become irate and as he raved his spittle struck Ricochet's face.

Ricochet grabbed the bum by the lower part of the lapels on his grimy, button-less, plaid sports coat. He slammed the bum against the brick wall. "Look old man, all we want is a few answers. And we're going to get them! So, if you don't start singing like a canary with a cattle prod up its rear end, I'll put my size eleven boot so far up <u>your</u> rear end that the water on my knee will quench your thirst!" Ricochet's face was so close that the bum should have been able to smell what Ricochet had had for breakfast two days ago.

He pinned the bum so hard against the wall the plaid jacket blended in with the brick pattern. Taking short and quick breaths, the bum attempted to get as much air as possible. Ricochet had effectively decreased the old bum's lung capacity by pressing him against the brick wall and jamming his fist into his chest.

"I don't sweat you!" the bum retorted, struggling, trying to break Ricochet's grip.

"Look, just cooperate and you'll be on your way," Rusty said.

"Mortimer Duke—Sergeant—United States Army-372805112," the bum sarcastically recited as if he were a prisoner of war.

Ricochet relaxed his grip just enough to let Mortimer slide off the brick wall. Then he quickly slammed him back against the wall. He applied pressure to his chest again, this time feeling something hard in Mortimer's breast pocket. Thinking it was a gun, Ricochet slammed him to the ground. The bum's protruding shoulder blades absorbed the initial brunt. Jamming his forearm against Mortimer's neck, Ricochet applied increasing pressure, forcing out all the air in his lungs. Mortimer appeared to be unconscious. Searching frantically with his free hand, Ricochet looked for the hidden weapon. No weapon was found. What he had thought to be a weapon was actually, not one, but two pint-size liquor bottles, one in each inside breast pocket.

Relieved, he released his grip on Mortimer, but not before confiscating the bottles. "You mean you almost had me break your fool neck, for a couple of liquor bottles?" Ricochet said, disgusted. He threw one of the bottles against the brick wall. It shattered violently upon impact.

Immediately, Mortimer jumped up, coughing and pleading, "No, no, not my tonic! Don't do it. I'll do anything." Ricochet, knowing he had Mortimer's undivided attention, began to taunt him.

"Oh, now you'll cooperate? What's different now than it was a few minutes ago?" Smiling crookedly, Ricochet began to toss the remaining liquor bottle from one hand to the other. "So, Dukey Boy, let's try this one more time. What's today's date, including the year? Where are we? And what time is it?" Ricochet faked throwing the bottle against the wall.

"I'll talk. I'll talk. Just, please, don't drop that bottle. Okay! Okay!" Dukey begged. "It's April 2, 1968. You're in an alley by Main Street and Simon Street. I don't know what time it is because I haven't had a watch in ten years, but the sun just went down a little while ago. All I know is it's almost nighttime. What else you want to know? I wear a size 38-suit jacket and size 10½ shoes. I had three wisdom teeth pulled when I was 19. And I stole a pack of cigarettes yesterday. But after I opened them I put them in my front pants pocket and went to sleep. When I woke up, I found out I peed on them. But I smoked them anyway."

This time, it was Ricochet's turn to shake his head and say, "Pit-a-ful!"

Mortimer continued, "Anything else you want to know?"

"Yeah, where's the Lorraine Motel?" Ham snarled.

Dukey, trying to divert his attention to Ham but never taking his eyes off the liquor bottle, told them they were only a few blocks from the motel. Satisfied with the answers, Ricochet told Mortimer Duke to get out of the alley, and then tossed the bottle into the air. Looking like Lynn Swann, a hall-of-famer wide receiver for the Pittsburgh Steelers, Mortimer dove with both arms and hands fully extended. He caught the bottle just before it hit the hard concrete, and cradled it, jubilantly. His elation lasted only a second, as he quickly collected himself and ran toward the end of the alley where he ran directly into Cliff. Mortimer's frail body crumpled upon impact with the solid police officer. Once again, he was on the concrete. And so was his bottle – broken into pieces. Mortimer scrambled onto his knees in a desperate hope of reclaiming some of the precious fluid. Using his tongue, he attempted to lap up the distilled fluid, but thought better of if when his tongue touched a broken piece of the glass bottle. He burst into tears. When he realized everyone was watching him, he wiped his face with his hands and stood up. Straightening his clothes, he exited the alley with his head held high, disappearing around the corner.

"Who in the Grant Hill was that?" asked Cliff, turning back from watching Mortimer flee from the alley.

"Not important. Report!" said Julian.

Without hesitation and enthusiastically, Cliff explained exactly where they were, confirming what Mortimer had just told them. Cliff had also located an abandoned warehouse where they could hide the time machine and use as a base of operations.

CHAPTER 8

"Cease fire! Cease fire! Cease fire, I said!" Special Agent Aubrey Pugh shouted, attempting to be heard over gunshot sounds and ricocheting bullets. Agent Pugh, who had been an FBI agent for over twenty years, was on the path toward retirement. He was a dedicated agent, who without any hesitation would gladly die for his country. However, over the last few years his job had become more of a tedious routine than an adventure.

Agent Aubrey Pugh, passed up several times for promotion, had an exemplary record. He was good at what he did. He just had not gotten any of the choice assignments, like some of the other agents, who were either related to or married to someone important in Washington D.C. When he was briefed on this assignment, he thought because of its importance to national security his luck and career would finally take an upswing before he retired.

Finally, Pugh thought, he would do something that would have a great impact on national security, and his name would be all over the report. He knew he would surely get a promotion out of it. It almost seemed too easy. All he had to do was stop Dr. Barnes from traveling back into time, confiscate that time machine, and then deliver it to the government. But, he saw his dream literally fade right before his very eyes when Julian and the others faded into the past.

The gunshots finally stopped. Bill, who had been hiding behind a piece of machinery, revealed himself again. "Man! We had them!" Agent Pugh uttered, contemptuously.

"Look at this place! You guys destroyed it," protested Bill. Actually, the condition of the laboratory was not too bad. Some minor arcing, sparking and smoke was the evidence that bullets had hit some of the equipment. But only a few pieces of equipment were damaged beyond repair. Agent Pugh hadn't been listening to

Bill complaining. He was too busy thinking of how he had failed his mission before it had really started. His attention was also diverted to his men; they attended to the agent accidentally shot by a stray bullet. He would require medical attention but he was going to be all right.

"Barnes is gone, and there is nothing we can do about it," said Agent Pugh, hinting hatred in his voice. Turning to his subordinates, Agent Pugh started barking orders.

Bill interrupted, much to the delight of the subordinates, " We can do something about it. There is another time machine."

Stopping in mid-sentence, Agent Pugh spun toward Bill. "What do you mean?" he asked.

"There is another one," Bill said. He led the FBI agents to a dimly lit storage room. When they entered, the first thing Agent Pugh noticed, besides weak incandescent lighting, was the odor of mildew and dampness. It smelled like his grandmother's house, as if a thousand wet rags were decaying. Then, completely covered by a white sheet, he saw what could only be another time machine.

Once Bill had completely unveiled the prototype unit to the other agents, Agent Pugh started caressing the time machine. He could once again think positively about his future.

This was the first time machine ever built. Every time they tested it, Julian and Bill had found a lot of mistakes in its design. A lot of travel hours had been logged on it, causing a low life in the Duracellium power pack. So rather than keep repairing it, they had built a new model.

"Well, what are we waiting for? Let's get this thing fired up and out of here!" Agent Pugh yelled.

"Wait a minute!" Bill retorted. "I run the show in here. If I try to move that unit and *fire it up*, as you say, before I purge it out with a molecular desiccant, we'll end up frying every circuit in there. Then we won't have a time machine at all."

Pugh looked at Bill as if he had lobsters coming out of his ears. Bill examined the unit. Under ideal circumstances, it would take about twelve hours to repair the unit. However, because of the damaged equipment in the laboratory, it would probably take about eighteen hours. But it would still lack the proper power supply.

Duracellium was a rare item in the 21st century. It was a powerful power source that combined the basic technology of the old alkaline batteries with nuclear fusion. The result was a non-polluting portable power source that would normally last for ten years. However, when used excessively, the life would drastically drop to two years. The government, due to heavy lobbying from large corporations and the limited supply of Duracellium, had kept tight control on the manufacturing and distribution of the product.

When presented with this dilemma, Agent Pugh informed Bill, "Don't worry about the Duracellium. Just get the machine fixed. I'll get you your Duracellium. I have friends who owe me favors."

He sent several agents to retrieve the Duracellium, and the others to take the injured agent to the hospital, while he stayed behind with Bill. He had already been left behind once by a time machine. He didn't intend to be left behind a second time.

CHAPTER 9

Meanwhile in the twentieth century:

Once they had moved the Time Machine and all the equipment into the abandoned warehouse, Julian went to work. There was no power being supplied to the warehouse so he cross-connected the Duracellium power pack to the building wiring. Although this was required, it was still very risky. The Duracellium power pack could be recharged from 110 to 120 volts but it would take hours to accomplish this task. Therefore, if the Time Team had to evacuate in an emergency, they would most definitely be in serious trouble. Previously, in the nineteenth century, this had not been a concern because they had not used the Time Machine to supply power to a building.

Once the lights were illuminated, they revealed a filthy, rat-infested environment. Certainly, at one time this had been the home of someone down on his or her luck. The empty Campbell's soup and Alpo dog food cans, liquor bottles and hundreds of cigarette butts, in which not a speck of tobacco remained, scattered randomly over the floor helped paint that picture. There was also a long table against a far wall, which was probably used as a bed.

"Give me a hand," Julian requested, attempting to pull the table away from the wall. At once, the others helped. The table was filthy and cluttered. Julian began cleaning it with a rag he had picked off the floor. He advised the others to follow suit with the rest of the place, since this was going to be their home for the next two days.

When the room was as close to clean as it was going to get, they laid the plans for the mission on the table and went over them several times. Julian was amazed at the way in which everyone understood and retained the plans, especially Ham and Ricochet.

Now, it was the third of April. Up until now, the Time Team had continued to prepare for the rest of the mission. Although it was 3:00 p.m. in the twentieth century, it was 3:00 a.m. in the twenty-first. And most of the team had gotten very little, if any, sleep. Satisfied everyone knew what was to happen the next day, Julian stopped the training. Motioning, he said to Cliff, "Let's go. We don't want to miss this." He didn't have to say where they were going. Everyone knew. "We'll be back tomorrow morning. Don't forget to turn off the power from the Duracellium pack. You'll never know when we might have to leave in a rush."

After they exited, everyone scrambled to find a comfortable spot to sleep. There was some light group conversation once the lights were secured. Ricochet wondered out loud, what the world would be like in the 21st century, if Dr. King *were* still alive. But, lack of sleep and the physical demands on their bodies during time travel had taken their toll on all of them. One by one, they drifted to sleep.

Exiting the building, Julian and Cliff turned right and headed south on South Main Street. They had brought a map with them but the route to the Lorraine Motel was simple enough to remember. The temperature had dropped about fifteen degrees since their arrival. Instinctively, they placed their hands into their pockets. The wind had also picked up fiercely, causing the few raindrops in the air to sting like pebbles. Julian quickly placed one hand onto his hat as it began to blow away. They were dressed fairly well for the weather; yet, the sudden temperature drop and gale force winds took some time for them to adjust to.

Cliff's thin tie and dark, narrow, straight leg pants fluttered back with the wind, emphasizing the contrast between the thinness of his legs and the large size of his feet.

They were in a run-down part of town, but everything was vivid and cheerfully touched them in living color. The only thing gloomy was the sky, for it had gotten very dark, very quickly. Of course, the setting of the sun did have something to do with this, but the sky was definitely turning a shade of storm-black.

As they made their way to the motel they saw no one on the streets. Anyone with good sense was not out in that weather, unless they had a good reason. There were probably only a few good reasons to be on the streets on that stormy night of April 3, 1968, in Memphis, Tennessee. To save the life of Dr. Martin Luther King, Jr. was definitely one of them, Julian thought.

Julian and Cliff walked for several minutes maintaining a good pace, although Cliff had to catch up with Julian every now and then. As they approached the intersection of Huling Avenue and South Street, Julian slowed his pace. They were walking on the west side of the street. As they got approximately one-third of the way down the street, Julian stopped and looked across. Not sure of what he was looking at, Cliff did the same. They were standing right across the street from Jim's Grill. It was below the boarding house where, from a back upstairs window, James Earl Ray had shot Dr. King.

The raindrops suddenly became larger and angrier as they beat heavily upon the aluminum awnings of some of the businesses. The storm had quickly developed into a torrential downpour, with the winds reaching dangerous speeds. It was as if the sky had come to life. Now, oblivious to the weather and most of his surroundings, Julian crossed the street to look inside the grill. Loud, heavy horns and screeching tires of large, oversized cars sounded, orchestrating with the sound of the hard falling rain and muffled sounds of motorists yelling and swearing through rolled-up car windows. However short, and perhaps unappreciated, it was a symphony in the rain, as a usually observant Julian did not look before crossing the street. Again, Cliff followed him.

Julian may have been somewhat oblivious, but he was not a dummy. He made sure he stopped *under* the awning as he looked inside the building. But that was only somewhat effective, as now the heavy raindrops were blowing horizontally. Julian saw only a few people inside; all were white. Some people, probably employees, looked as though they were preparing for a storm. Others sat and sipped beverages while staring outside the window, changing focal lengths only briefly when Julian stepped into view. Then, with a look of dismissal and disdain, they looked past Julian toward the street as if he didn't exist.

Walking further down the street became harder as the wind picked up. Several garbage cans, now acting as urban tumbleweeds, were blown into the streets by the fierce winds. They clamored loudly until they came to rest against buildings or parked cars. The contents of the rolling garbage cans were spewed wildly across the streets and into the gutters, further evidence the sanitation workers were on strike. Before coming to rest, some of the trash was caught in a twirling cyclonic updraft. Julian and Cliff stopped at other buildings on the same block and peered into their windows also. Just before they got to Butler Avenue, they turned left onto the sidewalk that arched around Fire Station #2. They began to jog, but because of the weather this quickly escalated to a sprint.

Now, they stood in the tornado level winds and rain, on the third floor balcony, in front of Room 306. Petrified, Cliff and Julian didn't move. They knew who was behind that door. Cliff seemed more awestruck than Julian. They had two choices: stand outside and inevitably catch pneumonia, or simply, "Knock so the door may be opened." At first, Julian tapped lightly, four times. It was so light he could barely hear it himself. He thought, "God, a mosquito in traction could knock louder than that."

They waited for ten seconds. Julian was about to knock harder. He coiled his fist back, preparing to wrap on the door, but the door suddenly opened, catching him completely off guard.

A brown-skinned man with a smooth bass voice opened the door. "Gentlemen, what brings you out on a night like this? The

153

weatherman says tornadoes have already been sighted and have touched down in some places. They recommend no one be out tonight unless it is an extreme emergency."

Julian and Cliff stood in the weather, awestruck, their mouths wide open.

"Speak up, gentlemen or I'm going to have to excuse myself and say good-bye. There's a lot of work to be done in the communities; I don't intend to be bed-ridden with the flu anytime soon," Dr. King said.

Reverend Ralph Abernathy, who had been in the motel room working with Dr. King, got up to see if he could lend any assistance. On many occasions, Reverend Abernathy had warned Dr. King about opening his doors. Deeply concerned about the safety of his friend, Reverend Abernathy inquired, with a certain irritation in his voice, *"Can we help you?"*

This snapped Julian out of his state of shock. "I'm so very sorry, sirs. I'm just so overwhelmed to meet you, Sir. I never dreamt it would be possible to meet you Sir," Julian confessed.

Julian could tell they were beginning to lose patience with him, especially Reverend Abernathy. So, he quickly changed gears. "Sir," Julian said, looking directly at Dr. King, "It is absolutely imperative that we talk to you. We're reporters from the *Detroit News*. I'm JJ Baines and this is my assistant, Cleveland Rhett." They exchanged handshakes and then Dr. King invited them in out of the weather.

"Take off your wet coats, gentlemen, and have a seat," Dr. King requested, smiling warmly. "You know, gentlemen, I would have invited you in, out of the weather, a lot sooner if only you had introduced yourselves and shaken my hand a lot sooner. So . . . what brings young brothers like yourselves all the way from Detroit, especially on a night like this?"

"Well, Sir, we'd like to have an interview with you, Sir. That is, if it's all right with you, Sir," Julian said, desperately hoping for a positive response.

However, before Dr. King could answer, Ralph Abernathy spoke up, "I'm afraid not, gentlemen. Dr. King is very tired, and he needs some rest. He has a full agenda tomorrow. In fact, I'm going to be filling in for Dr. King at his speaking engagement at the Masonic Temple tonight so he can get that rest."

Cliff commended Ralph Abernathy on his bravery for going back out into the weather, as now it felt and sounded like the building they were in would blow away.

"Ralph, let's not be so hasty. These men have come a long way from the North, from good ole Detroit," Dr. King paused, "And on a bad night like tonight. The least we can do is show them some good 'ole southern hospitality,'" He turned to Julian and Cliff saying, "We'll talk for a little while. And calm down; I've never been called 'Sir' that many times in my life, at least not in one sentence. I'm regular folk like yourselves." Dr. King smiled, getting up to get his guests some coffee.

Now, it was Ralph Abernathy's turn to smile, for he knew his long-time friend very well. As soon as Dr. King said they would talk for a little while, he shook his head in disbelief. Very rarely did Dr. King have short conversations with anyone.

Reverend Abernathy was also genuinely concerned about Dr. King's stamina and health. He knew Dr. King needed the rest. But, looking at his watch, Reverend Abernathy became alarming aware of the time. He hurriedly donned his coat and hat, and then bade good-bye to Julian and Cliff. Dr. King and Ralph Abernathy exchanged a masculine hug and bade each other good-bye.

Giving Julian and Cliff a cup of coffee, Dr. King sat down on the edge of his bed, facing the two time travelers, who sat on the sofa. Julian started by saying, "I like to first say it is a honor and a privilege to sit before you, Dr. King."

King responded, "Call me Martin, please. Like I said before, 'I'm just regular people, like everyone else.'"

Pulling out a mini-disc recorder, Cliff asked Dr. King if he minded if he recorded their conversation. The mini recorder immediately got Dr. King's attention. Picking it up, Dr. King examined it. He asked, "They make tape recorders *this* small?" Cliff started to point out that it was a disc, not a tape recorder. But Julian deliberately cut him off.

"It's amazing. Isn't it? What will those Japanese think of next?" Julian interjected, hoping that would satisfy Dr. King for a while.

The plan was for Julian and Cliff to spend as much time with Dr. King as possible so Dr. King and his staff would begin to trust them. Time flew by as the three talked about the Vietnam War, Dr. King's relationship with Malcolm X and also the possibility of Dr. King and Dr. Benjamin Spock running for president and vice president, respectively, later that year. Dr. King also covered with detail how he first decided to use the non-violent approach to fight segregation. He explained that he had read an essay in college, written in 1849 by a man named Henry David Thoreau. Thoreau believed a citizen had the right to disobey any law he or she thought was evil or unjust. Once, protesting slavery, Thoreau refused to pay his taxes. He was put in jail and a friend came to visit him.

"Why are you in jail?" his friend asked.

"Why are you out of jail?" Thoreau replied.

Other than Dr. King, his writings have influenced many leaders thriving to lead people toward justice and freedom, including the Danish Resistance during the 1940s, South Africans fighting against apartheid in the 1970s, and Mahatma Gandhi. Later, after hearing a speech about Gandhi, Dr. King was intrigued as to how Gandhi had won India's independence from the British in 1947 by using non-violent methods.

Pausing, Dr. King reflected on his time spent in the Birmingham jail cell and the letter he had written from there. He told of how he thought about the apostle Paul when he was in prison. He said he could feel Paul's pain and discouragement as Paul wrote Philippians 1:7 by the way Paul used the conjunction "or" instead of "and."

"Defending the gospel <u>and</u> being in chains should be synonymous, Dr. King preached. "But Paul quickly repented and found great encouragement from God, just six verses later, in verse thirteen. He then understood why he was in chains: to defend and confirm the gospel, only to a different audience. If only we, today's society, could repent that fast, the time it takes to write or read six verses," Dr. King remarked.

Dr. King went on to explain God also gave him strength during his incarceration, for he was greatly dismayed by criticism from some of the White religious leaders concerning his incarceration. They had remarked that perhaps he should have not gone to extreme measures and relegated himself to using a non-violent protest. Perhaps he was moving to fast, they had said. Dr. King recalled the excerpts he had written, in his letter, while in the Birmingham jail cell, to respond to those sentiments.

"I have almost reached the regrettable conclusion that the Negro's great stumbling block in the stride toward freedom is not the White Citizen's Councilor or the Klu Klux Klanner but the white moderate who is more devoted to order than justice; who prefers a negative peace which is the absence of tension to a positive peace which is the presence of justice. . . . I had also hoped that the white moderate would reject the myth of time. I received a letter this morning from a white moderate in Texas, which said,

'*All Christians know that the colored people will receive equal rights eventually, but is it possible that you are in too much of a religious hurry? It has taken Christianity almost 2000 years to accomplish what it has. The teachings of Christ take time to come to earth.*"'

"All that is said here grows out of a tragic misconception of time. It is the strangely irrational notion that there is something in the very flow of time that will inevitable cure all ills. Actually, time is neutral. It can be used either destructively or constructively . . . . We will have to repent in this generation not merely for the vitriolic words and actions of the bad people but for the appalling silence of the good people."

It had been over an hour and a half since they started talking. The mood had loosened up considerably. They were now joking and having fun. But Julian could tell Dr. King was fading fast, not so much by the occasional yawns he tried desperately to cover up, but because his speech had slowed down considerately. Dr. King was never a very fast talker, phonetically, but he was near perfect with his annunciation. Now, that had degraded. Julian felt guilty for keeping him up but he knew he had to talk to him for a little while longer, at least until the phone rang.

"It should have rung two minutes ago," Julian thought, checking his watch. "We've already changed the time line, probably because we delayed Ralph Abernathy."

Although expecting it, Julian was startled by the sound, which was harsh and crude compared with the soft ringers and computer announcing systems to which he had become accustomed.

Dr. King picked up the telephone and began to converse with the person on the other end. Although, both Julian and Cliff knew who it was and what the conversation was about, they listened intently. Dr. King said, "I'll be right there." Then hung up.

"That was Ralph." Dr. King explained. "It seems my presence is required at the Masonic Temple right now. I was due to speak there but because I was tired I decided to send Brother Ralph in my place. He just informed me several tornadoes have damaged towns in Arkansas, Tennessee and Kentucky. Also, several people have been killed in the storm and over one hundred injured. Yet, despite all of this, Ralph informed me thousands braved the elements and showed up. He said he tried to talk to them, but they didn't come to hear him. They came to hear me."

"So gentlemen, I hate to cut our conversation short, but I must go." Dr. King paused. "You know gentlemen, I must tell you, talking with you men was so different. I've talked to hundreds of reporters before . . . and I can't quite put my finger on it but there's a different air about you. It's as though your perspective is different than everyone else's." He paused, saying with a half smile, "Could it be you guys know something the rest of us don't know?"

Julian returned the half-smile and with a short burst of laughter, answering, "If we do, you'll read about it first in the *Detroit News*."

Dr. King added, "I would love to talk to you more at a later date. I'll tell you what, would you two like to join me this evening at the Temple? We can talk on the way." Without the slightest hesitation, Julian and Cliff accepted his invitation. This was part of the Time Team's original plans. They just hadn't known it was going to be that easy.

Walking out of the motel, the winds blew fiercely in an attempt to disrobe them. Instinctively, all of the men held tightly to their outer garments and grabbed their hats.

Dr. King turned around, walking backwards so the wind would hit his back instead of his face. Speaking over the high wind, he said, "If you men haven't booked a room, they are going to be hard to find. However, if we stop at the front desk, I'm sure I can convince Miss Lorraine to find you something here."

It was late when they arrived at the Masonic Temple. Their outer garments were soaking wet and their feet were cold. Dr. King was ushered through the back door; the same route Ralph Abernathy had taken. Following close behind in a single file, Julian and Cliff walked in the wake of three burly volunteer bodyguards.

As they inched their way to the side of the stage, Cliff thought the temple must have been packed many times over the fire code restriction. Then he wondered whether or not they had any such restrictions in the 60s.

Amazingly, amongst the hundreds of conversations going on and the sea of people in the Masonic Temple, someone recognized Dr. King while he was still making his way to the stage, and shouted, "He's here!" As if on cue, like tens of thousands of dominoes falling, all heads turned forward. There was a buzz within the crowd as Reverend Abernathy quickly introduced him. Then a loud, long, and thunderous cheer resounded.

The applause lasted for almost ten minutes. With no sign of faltering in sight, Dr. King turned, looking toward the side of the stage, he signaled the soundman. In response, the soundman turned up the volume to the old public address system. Dr. King then tapped the microphone, which resulted in an ear-wrenching and glass-shattering squeal. Instinctively, most of crowd reached up to cover their ears. This silenced them. Then he spoke.

"Thank you very kindly, my friends. As I listened to Ralph Abernathy in his eloquent and generous introduction and then thought about myself, I wondered who he was talking about." A low laugh rolled through the hall.

"It's always good to have your closest friend and associate to say something good about you. And Ralph is the best friend that I have in the world. I'm delighted to see each of you here tonight

160

despite the storm warning. You reveal that you are determined to go on anyhow. Something is happening in Memphis, something is happening in our world . . ."

The crowd responded with a roaring applause. Dr. King continued with his speech, talking about traveling back in time to visit other civilizations and societies.

Cliff elbowed Julian in his side. "It's alright," Julian said, responding to the non-verbal warning, but thinking, "Cliff has never heard Dr. King's, *I've been to the Mountaintop* speech. What are they teaching these young people in school these days?" The crowd hung on to every word Dr. King spoke.

" . . . I can remember, I can remember when Negroes were just going around as Ralph has said, so often scratching where they didn't itch, laughing when they were not tickled. But that day is over. We mean business now, and we are determined to gain our rightful place in God's world.

"And that's all this whole thing is really about. We ain't engaged in any negative protest and in any negative arguments with anybody. We are saying that we are determined to be men. We are determined to be people. We are saying that we are God's children. And that we don't want to live like we are forced to live."

The entire temple burst into triumphant applause. Despite the fatigue, Dr. King pressed on, talking for at least another hour. Finally, he shared a story about a letter he received from a little girl while he was in the hospital, after a demented woman stabbed him some years ago.

"I was rushed to Harlem Hospital. It was a dark Saturday afternoon. And the blade had gone through, and the x-rays revealed that the tip of the blade was on the edge of my aorta, the main artery. And once that's punctured, you drown in your own blood— that's the end of you."

"It came out in the *New York Times* the next morning that if I had sneezed, I would have died. Well, about four days later, they allowed me, after the operation, after my chest had been opened, and the blade had been taken out, to move around in the wheel chair in the hospital. They allowed me to read some of the mail that had came in. And from all over the states, and the world, kind letters came in."

"I read a few, but one of them I will never forget. I had received one from the President and the Vice President. I've forgotten what those telegrams said. I received a visit and a letter from the Governor of New York, but I've forgotten what the letter said. But there was one letter that came from a little girl, a young girl who was a student at White Plains High School. And I looked at that letter, and I'll never forget it. It said simply, 'Dear Dr. King: I am a ninth-grade student at the White Plains High School.' She said, 'While it does not matter, I would like to mention that I'm a white girl. I read in the paper about your misfortune, and of your suffering. And I read that if you had sneezed, you would have died. And I'm simply writing you to say that I'm so happy that you didn't sneeze.'"

There was a mixed response of applause, cheers, and awes. Cliff noticed Julian's eyes sparkle from wetness. Dr. King went on to say:

"And I want to say tonight, I want to say that I am happy that I didn't sneeze. Because if I had sneezed, I wouldn't have been around here in 1960, when students all over the South started sitting-in at lunch counters. . . . If I had sneezed I wouldn't have been around in 1962, when Negroes in Albany, Georgia, decided to straighten their backs up. And whenever men and women straighten their backs up, they are going somewhere, because a man can't ride your back unless it is bent."

The audience erupted in pandemonium, as hats were tossed into the air. Suddenly, there was a loud screeching noise. Dr. King gave the thumbs-up sign to the sound engineer once again. When the crowd noise subsided, Dr. King who was leaning more of his weight against the podium and whose speech had definitely slowed down, ended his speech.

"And they were telling me, it doesn't matter now. It really doesn't matter what happens now. I left Atlanta this morning, and as we got started on the plane – there were six of us – the pilot said over the public address system, 'We are sorry for the delay, but we have Dr. Martin Luther King on the plane. And to be sure that all of the bags were checked, and to be sure that nothing would be wrong with the plane, we had to check out everything carefully. And we've had the plane protected and guarded all night.' And then I got into Memphis. And some began to say the threats, or talk about the threats, were out. What would happen to me from some of our sick white brothers?

"Well, I don't know what will happen now. We've got some difficult days ahead. But it does not matter with me now. Because I have been to the mountaintop. And I don't mind. Like anybody, I would like to live a long life. Longevity has its place. But I'm not concerned about that now. I just want to do God's will. And He's allowed me to go up to the mountain. And I've looked over. And I've seen the promise land. I may not get there with you. But I want you to know tonight, that we, as a people will get to the promised land. And I'm happy tonight. I'm not worried about anything. I'm not fearing any man. Mine eyes have seen the glory of the coming of the Lord."

The Masonic Temple once again erupted into loud applause and cheering. Though the applause was thunderous, Julian sensed the cheering was not as loud as he had thought it would be for this great speech, especially if he used the earlier enthusiasm of the over-packed hall as a barometer. Surveying the crowd, he noticed perhaps one out of every four people either weren't clapping or just "show clapping." They seemed to sense an ulterior meaning hidden behind it. "Maybe Dr. King was just tired," Julian thought. But it seemed, although Dr. King had said he was happy and not worrying, his expression and tone told a different story. It appeared to Julian at least, that Dr. King might have known more about the events that were to occur in less than twenty-four hours. Julian thought, "I wonder if . . . ?"

CHAPTER 10

Six FBI agents entered the laboratory, reporting joyfully, "We've got the Duracellium, sir." Agent Pugh, who only moments before, had been sleeping propped against a large piece of laboratory equipment, awoke with a start and sprang to his feet.

It had been almost twelve hours since the agents had left to retrieve the Duracellium. During that time, Bill had been diligently at work repairing the older time machine and making preparations for their time travel attempt. He wanted very badly to be the one who stopped Julian. He was extremely tired but became energized when he saw the agents carrying the lead-lined container that housed the radioactive material. Agent Pugh eyed him with much concern.

"About six more hours," Bill announced. "Once I inject this into the cells, it will take about five hours to stabilize. Then, we're on our way," He weighed the contents of the lead container.

He reluctantly reported to Agent Pugh, "This is not enough Duracellium. We have enough to get us there, but not enough to get us back unless we get power from the other time machine."

"Well I guess we'll really need to find them once we get there," Agent Pugh snapped.

"You know, if for some reason we don't find them, we will be stuck in the 20th century," Bill responded.

"And your point being?" Pugh asked.

"Never mind," Bill said, turning toward the Duracellium to start the nuclear fueling process.

Following proper protocol for handling of nuclear material, Dr. Rousseau painstakingly replaced the old Duracellium. About one hour later, he reported to Pugh, "In order for the Duracellium to work properly, I must force an accelerated half-life by speeding up the natural decay rate. It will take about five hours for the cycle to complete. I have everything else ready to go. Right now, I really don't have anything else to do. So, I'm going into the control room to take a nap. The computer will wake me up when the Duracellium is ready."

Bill climbed the short steps leading up to the control room. He normally climbed the steps rapidly, taking two steps at a time. Today was different. His footsteps were heavier and he held on to the side rail for support.

Upon entering the control room, he sought the comfort of the soft leather chair. Before he sat down, he observed the FBI agents through the chromafilter control room glass. They stood in a semi-circle watching him through the control room glass. Bill pretended not to look in their direction. None of the agents spoke until the automatic door closer mounted on the door to the control room performed its job to satisfaction. Then they engaged in an intense conversation, occasionally looking at the control room to observe Bill, who had spun his chair around so the agents could not see him.

Discreetly, Bill pressed a button on the control panel. The label directly beneath the button read, "Lab Monitor." Almost precisely at the moment he pressed the button, his heart felt as though it had jumped through his rib cage. He scrambled to turn down the volume of the speaker to eliminate the feedback noise.

"Look I already told . . . ," said the electronically amplified voice of Agent Pugh. There was a slight pause and then he continued, "When we find Dr. Barnes, we must isolate him from the rest of the group and then kill him! You won't just shoot him. You will shoot to kill! Julian Barnes will not make it back to the 21st century alive. With him dead and out of the way it should be a cinch to convince Dr. Rousseau to head the government's time travel division."

Bill heard another pause in the monitored conversation. When the agents resumed, they had changed the subject completely. The monitor speaker did not generate the next sound Bill heard, nor was it familiar to him. It was the clicking sound of a revolver being cocked. The revolver was not the standard issue weapon of the Federal Bureau of Investigation. In fact, it was a far cry from the laser-assisted semi-automatic weapons they used, but the FBI agents were carrying weapons similar to the ones used in the 1960s.

Caught off guard, Bill said the first thing that came to mind. "Eavesdropping is by no means proper conduct for a gentleman. But no doubt the deed is already done." Upon feeling the cold hard steel from the barrel of the revolver pressing against the back of his head and hearing the click of its hammer, it was the only semi-intelligent thing he could think to say.

"How much did you hear, nosey boy?" demanded one of Pugh's agents, pushing the barrel of the gun harder against the ear of the scientist.

In a move unexpected by the agent, Bill slapped the gun away and responded angrily, "I heard enough to tell you I'm not going to take you back into time, so you can kill my frie..."

Bill didn't get to finish his last word. The agent grabbed him, pulled him to his feet and roughly hauled him out of the control room. Bill's protests fell upon deaf ears as the agent thrust him onto the floor in front of Agent Pugh. "He says he ain't taking us back in time, Sir," the agent reported.

No look of anger, surprise, or disappointment showed on Pugh's face. In fact, his face displayed no emotion at all. If ever there was a model poker face, Agent Pugh definitely displayed it – albeit briefly. There was something under the façade of his cool demeanor and poker face. Agent Pugh knelt down to where Bill had been thrown and helped him to his feet. Bill remained passive, not responding to Pugh's attempts to help. Pugh proceeded to straighten Bill's clothes, since the other agent had ruffled them. Turning, he rebuked the agent, "All this was not necessary!"

Agent Pugh then placed his arm around and upon Bill's shoulder, walking him away from the other agents. Pugh lowered his voice, saying, "I hate it when he does that."

Bill relaxed. With his arm still around Bill, Agent Pugh continued, "You know, Bill, if I don't go on this mission my career is essentially over, and probably my life as well. I will probably end up committing suicide—Bang, a bullet in the head!" he explained, putting his own gun to his head.

Nonchalantly replacing his gun back into the holster, Pugh continued, "So you see, Billy, if you don't take us back, I'm as good as dead. It's just a matter of time before I build up enough courage to do it. So, you see, Billy boy, I might as well kill you," he whispered, Bill feeling the heat of Agent Pugh's breath as he now talked directly into Bill's ear. "There's no need in you living and me dying. But, being the softy that I am, before I kill you, I'll probably give you one more chance. However, before any of that happens, I'm going to beat the livin' snot out of you."

Before Bill could protest or pull away, Pugh's arm tightened around him hard and quickly, like a giant pair of Vicegrips. Bill felt the pounding pain of a punch that had burrowed itself deep within his midsection. He saw it coming but had little time or the ability to defend himself because of the paralyzing grip Agent Pugh had around his shoulder. After delivering the blow, he released Bill, allowing him to double over in pain before collapsing to the floor. He then delivered a double-fisted sledgehammer blow to Bill's back. With each pounding blow, there was a combination of sounds of pain and the escape of air leaving Bill's body. He gasped for air while on his hands and knees, and then received a kick in the ribs that lifted him off all fours and onto his side. The once poker-faced Pugh now had a smirk on his face that turned into a smile; each blow he delivered excited him more.

Bill lay helpless, wheezing and gasping for air. He was fully aware of what was going on around him. He was getting the snot beat out of him. Then, as quickly and abruptly as the beating had begun, it ceased. Agent Pugh, now in a much calmer state, pulled out his gun and gently placed the end of the barrel directly against an eye of the scientist.

Immediately, Bill forgot about his other pains. He froze at the sight of the out-of-focus gun, and the feel of the cold steel against his eyelid. "Now Billy Boy, you will get this time machine ready. And you will take us back in time. Or, without a doubt, you will die today; today is a good day to die. And it will be in this room. I hope I've made myself crystal clear. Now, let me help you up."

Agent Pugh pulled his suit jacket back, and replaced his revolver into its holster. Bending over, he helped Bill to his feet. Bill withdrew slightly but thought it better not to resist any further. Pugh walked with his arm around Bill's shoulders, escorting him to the control room, just like they were old friends and nothing had happened.

"You be sure to get some good rest. I want you to be well rested for our trip," Agent Pugh urged. He stopped directly in front of the steps leading up to the control room. "Be careful on those steps," warned Agent Pugh. "I sure wouldn't want to see you get hurt."

Bill winced and nearly collapsed as Pugh playfully but purposely hit him lightly in a now tender spot of the rib section, where he was kicked. For Bill, the stairs were harder to ascend, more than he had ever experienced.

Pugh watched him ascend toward the control room. Turning toward one of his agents, he ordered, "Go baby-sit him. If he does anything peculiar, stop him. I don't care if he combs his hair against the grain; stop him! I don't trust him." The agent escorted Bill to the control room. Pugh turned his back, informing his other agents, "Okay gentlemen, get ready. We leave in four hours."

169

Not a word was exchanged between Bill and his unwanted escort. Painfully reclining in the office chair, Bill stared at the ceiling, silently praying for strength and wisdom to properly handle the situation. Then he fell into a deep sleep. While Bill dreamt, a look of satisfaction washed over his face. The FBI guard noticed, but did not care as long as Bill was asleep. But Agent Pugh was watching. He definitely didn't trust Bill, but he had needed him. If Pugh had not needed him, he would have already killed him.

*****

In his dream, Bill was at his high school prom with his date. She, a beautiful girl, had very long hair. Her hair was at least one hundred feet long and it was in seven braids, like Samson's hair. All the FBI agents were musicians, playing in a heavy metal band.

Agent Pugh, who was playing the lead guitar in the band, broke a guitar string. So, he reached out and plucked a hair from the head of Bill's date to use as a replacement. Suddenly, all seven braids of her hair came alive like the snakes of Medusa. Each braid wrapped around a FBI agent like a python, and choked, but did not kill them. As the braids attacked the agents, a spotlight from the tier shone brightly on each of them, blinding them.

In his second dream, Bill dreamt he was a weathervane, mounted on top of an old farmhouse. Rotating and squeaking as the wind changed directions, he finally steadied out and pointed, as if besieged by rigor mortis, in the direction the wind was blowing.

When Bill was awakened four hours later, he knew exactly what he must do.

*****

Agent Pugh unknowingly made a critical error before he, the droned agents, and Bill time traveled to 1968. He assumed he knew enough about time travel to control Bill. Because of that critical mistake, he made a second mistake. He did not wear the chromafilter glasses during the time travel. Bill just happened to forget to inform him of the need to wear them.

*****

Bill and the FBI agents materialized in the 20th century. However, Bill was the only one conscious, as he was the only one who had worn the chromafilter glasses.

" . . . forget you, and the horse you rode in on," Bill yelled, kicking Agent Pugh twice in the ribs. He would have punished Pugh a little more, but he was afraid he might wake him up.

Removing and pocketing his chromafilter glasses, a half smile developed on his face. He looked at the unconscious FBI agents, asking, "Did I do that? I'm sorry, it must have slipped my mind to tell you to put on the glasses before time traveling."

Fortunately for him, they had materialized in the same district Julian's team materialized in. As luck would have it, Bill and the FBI agents were directly in front of an abandoned building. It took minimal effort for Bill to drag everyone and everything into the building.

He glared at Agent Pugh, lying motionless and sprawled on the floor, with a feeling of satisfaction. He probably would have felt better if Pugh were conscious so he could feel pain from the kicks. Not wasting any more time, Bill took the seven ropes he had brought along and tied up each agent. This was the answer he had received in the first dream.

Bill then concentrated his efforts on his next task at hand. He opened the gray metallic box he had brought along and removed a neutron counter, typically used to test for radiation leakage from

Duracellium. It was a very sensitive instrument and would normally detect even the minutest amount of leakage. Agent Pugh had allowed Bill to bring it because their supply of Duracellium was limited and they didn't want to risk having any sort of leak.

However, Bill knew with a slight modification, he could use the neutron counter to locate Julian by detecting the Duracellium from Julian's time machine. This was the answer he had received in the second dream. His only concern now was how to get rid of Agent Pugh.

It took only a couple of minutes to modify the neutron counter, as only a few static adjustments had to be performed. The battery-operated, hand-held device came alive and registered a read-out on its small LED screen. After compensating for the Duracellium that was in the same room, Bill was able to get a directional fix on another source of Duracellium.

Leaving the building and the bound agents behind, he started on his mission to find Julian. He was one hundred percent sure the source he was tracking was Julian, since Duracellium had not yet been invented in the 1960s.

*****

It was a cool day on April 4, 1968. Julian and Cliff were just returning to the hideout. They had spent the last day with Dr. King. It had been a very productive time. They had grown very close to Dr. King and he to them. As they were about to open the door to the hideout, Cliff told Julian, "You know, I'd give my life to save Dr. King's life. I had no idea he was such a gentle and knowledgeable man. The world was definitely cheated when he was murdered."

Julian placed his hand on the loose and rusted doorknob. He gave it a half turn as he looked back at Cliff. "Remember your words," he responded, "You may have to do just that." He turned the doorknob its final half turn.

The door creaked on its hinges, as it swung open, revealing the dark chamber within. At first, Julian thought it odd that the room was dark. Then he dismissed that thought, thinking the others must have been trying to save the Duracellium power supply. Suddenly, the door slammed shut, darkening the room totally. Julian and Cliff were shoved face-down to the floor. Cliff recognized the metallic clicking sounds of firearms as they were being readied to shoot. Each man felt a knee in his back and a gun pressed to the back of his head. Both realized if the ambushers had intended to kill them, it would have happened as soon as the door was opened.

Suddenly, a bright flashlight was pushed before Julian's face. "Oh, it's you," Ricochet said, taking his knee out of Julian's back. He helped him to his feet. Ham followed suit, doing the same thing for Cliff.

"Who did you think we were?" Julian demanded.

Before Ham or Ricochet could answer, Rusty stepped from behind the doorway that led into a back room. Only, he was not alone. In front of him was Bill, bound and gagged.

Ham cocked his head, asking, "Any more questions?"

"What are you doing here? But I guess a better question is how did you get here?" As soon as Julian asked the second question, he knew the answer. "You fixed the old time machine, didn't you?" "But where did you get the Duracellium? Probably from the government, you worm! So where are those FBI agents? Did you bring them to crucify us, Judas?" Julian asked. Leaning toward Bill, Julian kissed him on the cheek.

Ham and Ricochet looked at each other. "It's biblical. I'll explain it to you later," Ham said, leaning toward Ricochet. Ricochet leaned away, in case Ham wanted to kiss him.

Pointing toward the floor, Julian continued, "Look, you dropped some of your silver coins."

Julian removed the gag and then looked at him with raised eyebrows as if to say, "What?"

As the two men stared at each other, Bill was at a loss for words. He wanted to tell Julian so badly, "I'm sorry for what I've done and I'm here to save your life." But he couldn't get it out.

Ricochet broke the silence. "Where are the FBI agents who were shooting at us, and what do you want?"

Turning toward Ricochet, Bill said, "They're a couple of blocks away!"

Ricochet shouted, furiously, *"See, I knew we couldn't trust him!"* Withdrawing his sidearm from his holster, in a quick and fluent motion, Ricochet pressed it against Bill's temple. "I say we waste his Benedict Arnold butt, right here, right now, and feed his carcass to the birds!"

Bill turned toward Ricochet, meeting his cold stare. For the moment, he tried desperately to forget about the loaded weapon pointed directly at his head. "But don't worry, they're all tied up now," he added. "And, I came to save Julian's life."

Bill updated the entire Time Team as to what had happened with the FBI, from the moment the team last saw the FBI agents, until the present. Julian was touched that his friend would risk so much to save him.

"So, my friend," Julian announced, "We are still going through with the mission. The question is, 'Where do you stand?'"

Bill paused before answering to choose the right words. He saw hatred in their eyes, especially in Ricochet and Ham's. The last thing Bill wanted to do, at that point, was to fuel additional hatred uttering some off the wall social remark.

Bill answered. "Due to recent events, I now am convinced society in the 21st century is not as perfect as I once believed. I have been shielded from the truth as much as I have been blinded by reality. If Dr. Martin Luther King, Jr. had lived, people would be different in the United States and probably in the world. Finding out the FBI had put into action a sinister plot to murder Julian opened my eyes. So, now that I've had an up close encounter with the FBI's corruption in the 21st century, it's easy for me to conclude the FBI in the 20th century was more-than-likely involved in the assassination of Dr. King, or at least knows more about it than they say." Pausing, he looked at everyone and then continued, "Plus, I lost sight of the real value of friendship and I'm here now to help my friends." One by one, he looked directly in their eyes, purposely looking at Ham last. Then he said, "I'M WITH YOU!"

In response, the small room filled with jubilation. Bill received several pats on the back and handshakes from everyone, except Ham.

Julian, who seldom missed much, noticed this. Looking at Bill's purple bruises and swollen lips, Julian asked, "What happened to you?"

"The FBI. I'll explain later," Bill muttered.

Once the mini-reunion had subsided, Julian revised the plans for saving Dr. King. Julian and Cliff still would stay close to Dr. King, guarding him. But, with the introduction of the new players, Ricochet and Rusty were assigned to guard the FBI agents. This left Ham and Bill. They were assigned the all-important task of stopping James Earl Ray: the man accused of killing Dr. King.

Ham's expression hardened even more, with the announcement of the pairing of the last two members of the Time Team. Julian had a good reason to put Ham and Bill together. Even though he believed Bill was sincere when he said he was with them, he knew Ham could handle Bill if that were not the case. Also, since Ham did not care for Bill, Julian wanted to give them the opportunity to develop trust for each other. The Time Team would be unsuccessful without trust between all the members. The only question was how far would Ham go if he discovered Bill was still working with the FBI.

Julian got his answer shortly. Pulling Julian aside, Ham whispered to him in a low and very heavy voice. "At the first sign of him turning traitor," he paused, "I will kill him."

Caught completely off guard by the remark, Julian asked, "You're joking, right?"

Ham looked Julian directly in the eyes, without wavering, and ended the conversation by saying, "We shall see. But I will bring the body back for you." Turning, Ham walked away.

CHAPTER 11

It was still April 4, 1968, but now the time was 6:01 in the evening. Only adrenaline prevented the two time travelers from panting heavily as they raced up the old stairs, toward the bathroom of the boarding house. Ham and Bill had been running for blocks, trying to make it there in time. Neither of them were in the best shape, especially Bill. Yet, they persevered, knowing the time for the shooting of Dr. King was rapidly approaching.

They would have arrived ten minutes earlier, but were detained by a Memphis police officer. Ham had just rounded the corner at Vance Street and South Main Street. Bill, who was a much slower runner, tried his best to keep up, yet he still fell behind, even when Ham slowed his pace. But, Ham made sure Bill saw every turn he made. He didn't want to lose him along the labyrinthine route.

"Come on!" Ham yelled, continuously motioning with his arm for Bill to catch up before he reached South Main Street. "I've got a dead grandmother that moves faster than you. And she's been cremated!" Ham shouted.

He picked up speed once again and then spilled out onto South Main Street, while still looking back for Bill. As he did, he ran directly into a police officer. "Oomph!" Both expelled, hitting each other, before hitting the ground. Unfortunately for Ham, the police officer recovered before he did.

"What's your hurry, Boy?" the officer demanded, slightly disoriented. "Where you runnin' to? Or should I say, from what?" Pulling his gun out of its holster, the policeman ordered Ham to his feet. "Up! Git up on your feet, Boy!"

Focusing on the barrel of the drawn weapon, Ham tried to stand, but stumbled. He soon felt his entire body being thrust against a nearby brick wall. Ham was barely able to sidestep the garbage can that sat next to the wall.

"Spread em, Boy! Hands above your head. Let's see what you stole," the policeman said, searching through Ham's pockets.

"I didn't steal anything; I'm sorry for running into you officer," Ham apologized.

"Don't you sass me, Boy!" the police officer responded, harshly. Ham turned his head slightly over his left shoulder in order to get a look at the officer's name and badge. "Turn back around, Boy. Don't breathe 'less I tell ya, don't' move 'less I tell ya. And when I tell you to move, Boy, you better ask me, 'To what state?'" Officer Stone ordered, while pressing his gun barrel deep into the flesh at the base of Ham's skull.

Officer Stone continued the search. "Now let's see if you got anything on you." Ham glanced at his watch. He was running behind schedule. At that exact same time, Officer Stone found the weapon Ham had strapped to his side, inside his long coat. "Well, lookee here. This must be my lucky day. I think I hit the jackpot. I found myself a rebel boy," Stone remarked, pausing to inspect the weapon, "I neva seen this type of gun before." The mysterious assault weapon now distracted him totally.

Sensing this was his window of opportunity, Ham decided to jump through it, no matter how small it was. He quickly stole a glance at the garbage can at his immediate left. It was within arm's length. In one quick motion, Ham spun around, snatching the shiny aluminum top to the garbage can; he used it to hit the assault weapon. The weapon leapt out of Stone's hand like a large, black, metallic grasshopper.

It created a hot, golden spark as it hit the gray, chalky, concrete sidewalk at an obtuse angle. Skidding along the sidewalk for another six feet, it came to rest out of the immediate reach of Officer Stone. Stone had been caught off guard but recovered quickly. He immediately brought the revolver in his right hand directly into Ham's face.

"Oh! Now you wanna hit White people with garbage can tops. You shouldn't have done that, boy! Now I gotta kill ya," Stone said, joy in his voice. Ham slowly retreated backwards toward the cold, hard, brick wall. Hitting the wall, he now had no other direction to go, except forward, directly into the gun.

Bill rounded the corner. Although slower, he was extremely light on his feet. He moved silently. Seeing the situation unfolding right in front of him, Bill realized every precious moment was critical if both Dr. King and Ham were to escape the destinies that were seconds away.

Bill ran toward Stone, who had his back to him. He launched himself, pulling his gun out of his holster while in mid-flight.

The distance between Bill and Officer Stone closed rapidly. When he got arm's length away from Stone, he drew his arm back, bringing a mighty blow to the back of the policeman's head. Like a human house of cards, Officer Stone collapsed onto the ground. Only a split second before, Ham had squinted his eyes and dulled his ears in anticipation of a gun blast and instant death. The Memphis policeman's brain had already sent the electrical impulse to his finger. He started to squeeze the trigger. Ham knew this was the end.

Stone was obstructing Ham's vision. He did not know Bill was flying toward them until he saw Stone unconscious on the sidewalk, with Bill on top of him. "About time you got here!" Ham said, trying to conceal the quivering of his voice. "My grandmother's ashes blew by a few minutes ago."

"You're welcome," Bill responded, picking himself off the ground, "I've got no time to make you humble. We've got a job to do." Turning, he took off running in the direction of the boarding house. Ham started to run after Bill but stopped abruptly in his tracks. He grabbed Stone by his ankles and pulled him into the alley, out of sight, before retrieving his gun. He caught up with Bill as they reached the boarding house.

Looking at his watch, Bill slowed down only enough to enter the door. Ham ran right up to Bill's back, panting heavier because of his two-block-long sprint. Bill saw the time and worried, although, they knew they weren't too late because neither one of them had heard a shot.

It was 6:01 in the evening. Only adrenaline prevented the two time travelers from panting heavily as they raced up the old stairs, toward the bathroom of the boarding house.

They were cutting it close, real close. The sniper had been set up in the bathroom for sometime and was prepared to shoot. His only delay was in awaiting the arrival of Dr. King on the balcony of his motel room.

With one eye glued to the powerful telescope affixed to the top of the hunting rifle, and his right index finger set loosely on the trigger, the sniper waited patiently for his target. He knew the time was near. He began to synchronize his breathing so his shot would be true. He had obviously done this before. He had nerves of steel and the concentration of a lioness as she stalks her prey.

"Ah-hah," the sniper exclaimed, seeing Dr. King exit his motel room. He knew his painful patience would pay off. He attempted to line up the crosshairs in the scope's viewer with Dr. King's head. At first, because the men leaving with Dr. King were doing a good job of shielding and shadowing him, the sniper was unable to line up a clear shot. Then, without warning, one of Dr. King's men abruptly turned around and headed back in the direction of the motel room.

The sniper took full advantage of this opportunity. He locked onto the human target like a hungry hawk in flight spotting a field mouse. And much like the Memphis police officer, the gunman's brain sent the necessary electrical impulse from the brain to the finger to squeeze the trigger. Only this time the result was much different. The signal was not short-circuited.

Ham and Bill had weapons drawn as they ascended the stairs. They never considered slowing down when they reached the top of the stairs and saw the "Out of Order" sign hanging on the bathroom door.

Still running at top speed, the two time travelers, simultaneously, took one last deep breath. Since both were solid men, they rammed into the door like a couple of human wrecking balls. The bathroom door exploded off its hinges, sending wood chips and plaster from the doorframe into the air. It fell back into the bathroom and splintered against the brown-stained and dirty, porcelain toilet bowl. Although very loud, the crashing sound of the door was not loud enough to mask the sound of exploding gunpowder within the rifle's chamber.

The sniper whipped his head in the direction of the now broken door. It took a full second for his brain to register exactly what had happened. That was long enough for Ham and Bill to seize an advantage. Quickly, they overtook the startled sniper before he could pull the rifle barrel back through the window and aim the deadly weapon at them. Grabbing the sniper, they threw him face down to the floor.

"Don't move or I'll blow your fool head off," Ham shouted to the back of the sniper's head, pinning him down with one knee driven into his back.

"Hurry up, man. Let's get out of here. The police are probably on their way!" Bill exclaimed.

With that, Ham nodded, and with the butt of the gun leading the way, he delivered a blow to the back of the sniper's head.

Blackness instantly overtook the sniper's mind. He was knocked out cold. Ham rolled him over to check for a pulse and made a startling and chilling discovery. The discovery wasn't the sniper was dead; he was alive, just very unconscious and bleeding from the back of the head.

181

"This ain't James Earl Ray!" Ham announced. In fact, neither Ham nor Bill had any idea who the man was. All they knew was this man tried to kill Dr. Martin Luther King Jr., and unless they wanted to spend the rest of their lives in a twentieth-century prison, they had to leave quickly.

Ham knelt beside the unconscious man, trying to make heads or tails of what was happening. "We don't have time for this; we have to leave yesterday! Finish it!" Bill reminded Ham. Picking up the unknown gunman by the front of his jacket and the hair on the top of his head, Ham pulled him toward the scum-stained toilet bowl. Using the unconscious man's hair as a handle, he rubbed the back of his head on the front and top edge of the toilet, thus transferring blood onto it. He dropped the gunman to the floor, in front of the toilet, and placed the broken door on top of him. Then, as quickly as Ham and Bill were on the scene, they departed, just seconds before the police stormed the building.

As they fled, Ham and Bill had two questions in their head. First, who in the world was that sniper if he wasn't James Earl Ray? Second, was the crashing sound of the door enough to disturb the sniper so he had missed his mark?

James Earl Ray had been proclaiming his innocence for decades before his death in prison. He had maintained he was framed and not guilty of the crime that caused the whole world to mourn.

CHAPTER 12

It was a cold, breezy and gray day. Although not visible through the cloud cover, the sun was just about to set over the horizon. Julian stood at the open door to Dr. King's motel room. He was waiting for them to exit, but trying everything he could think of to delay them. Julian was growing more anxious. He knew what day it was and what time it was. It was April 4th, and almost 6:00 P.M.

He glanced across the street, periodically, toward the window of the boarding house. Unfortunately, all he could see was that the window was open. Regardless of the lack of light and distance, he should have been able to see the powerful flashlight Bill was to shine once they had subdued James Earl Ray. "What are they on, C.P. time?" Julian asked Cliff, as they stood in the open doorway.

Dr. King overheard the remark and looked up from where he sitting. Staring at Julian oddly, Dr. King's eyes were larger than normal while they spoke. "Okay, gentlemen, let's go," Dr. King said, "We don't want to be late."

Dr. King, his staff, Julian and Cliff exited Room 306 and walked along the balcony, toward the stairs, leading to the ground floor of the Lorraine Motel. Men in the front, rear and both sides surrounded Dr. King. He could hear, but could not see the crowd that had gathered below the balcony just to get a glimpse of the famous civil rights leader. The group of men dressed in black overcoats stepped onto the balcony. At first the crowd went silent when they could not see Dr. King. Then the crowd began to buzz. And the buzz grew to a roar. Somehow they could sense Dr. King was within the group of men.

Suddenly, Reverend Abernathy, who was on the right side of Dr. King, turned and headed back toward the motel room, saying, "I'm going to need my sweater."

Dr. King's right side was now exposed. Like a volcano, a very loud roar erupted from below, as Dr. King was now exposed to the crowd as well. They waved, cheered and called out his name in a triumphant and jubilant approval. In response, Dr. King stopped and leaned over the balcony. He waved back at his followers.

Julian, who had been walking in front of Dr. King, turned his head and saw what was going on. Sensing the imminent danger, he felt a cold wave of fear shoot up his spine. He immediately turned his whole body and lunged toward Dr. King, yelling, "Nooooo!" But it was too late.

Dr. King's collapse was only a few milliseconds out of sync with a loud firecracker-like sound, which emanated from across the parking lot at the boarding house. His staff quickly surrounded him. Lowering himself to one knee, a young staff member named Andrew Young pointed toward an open window at the boarding house.

"Call an ambulance!" someone screamed. But this plea could barely be heard over the hysterical crowd.

Julian and Cliff held Dr. King down as he rolled around in obvious pain. Julian saw a hole in the upper left shoulder of Dr. King's overcoat. He looked at Cliff and pleaded with him, "Can you do anything for him?"

Julian knew Cliff was not a physician or a medic. But being a cop, he hoped he had some experience with gunshot wounds. Cliff reached into one of his pockets, producing a red Swiss Army knife. Dr. King's eyes opened wide. "I've just been shot, now I'm going to get stabbed," he thought.

Cliff brought the short shiny blade toward the bullet wound. When all the surrounding clothing had been cut away from the wound, it revealed what Cliff had expected. The wound was only superficial. "It's only a flesh wound. It barely nicked the shoulder," Cliff reported. Scanning the outside wall of the motel, he found what he had been looking for, a bullet hole. Apparently, the high velocity bullet must have nicked Dr. King's shoulder and continued on, with only a minor deflection off its path toward and through the motel wall.

"It's okay to move him. Let's get him out of here!" Cliff suggested. They formed a human barrier around Dr. King, rushing him back into the motel room as if they were one unit.

CHAPTER 13

It had been almost three hours since the attempt on Dr. King's life. He had been rushed back into his motel room. His entourage stood in a semi-circle around the bed. Everyone had a look of concern coupled with relief when the doctor gave his final diagnosis. "You were lucky . . . real lucky. Another couple of inches this way or that way and the bullet would have caused irreparable damage to a main artery, which means you would have died within seconds," the doctor concluded.

"I heard on the car radio, on the way here, the police have caught the guy," the doctor said, continuing to dress the wound. "They said they found him in the bathroom of that boarding house building across the parking lot. They said, apparently the dumb fellow took the shot from a bathroom window and panicked. The bathroom door must have been locked and in his state of mind he must have ripped the door off its hinges, right onto his head. When he fell backwards, he hit his head on the toilet knocking himself out."

Immediately after the doctor stopped speaking, there was a noise at the door as someone tried to open the locked door. Silence fell upon the small motel room as everyone turned to look at the door. There was the sound of a key being inserted into the lock Dr. King sat on the edge of the bed, unnerved. The doctor stood silently beside him, a roll of gauze in his hand. He had been wrapping Dr. King's shoulder, but he, like everyone else in the room had stopped what they were doing in anticipation of what was going to happen next. Julian, Cliff, Reverend Abernathy and two other men moved quickly to form a human shield in front of Dr. King and the doctor.

The door swung open and the largest man Julian had ever seen stepped into the motel room. Walking toward them, he looked down at Cliff and Julian.

Behind this hulk, standing in the doorway was a lovely, petite Black woman. "Hold it, Don. They're with us." Dr. Abernathy exclaimed, hurriedly. The large man stopped, immediately.

"What is it, Ralph?" Dr. King asked.

Before Dr. Abernathy could answer, a higher pitched voice called out. "Martin!" Coretta Scott King ran through the shield of men separating her from her husband. They parted as evenly and symmetrically as the Red Sea, allowing Coretta to reach her husband. She hugged him tightly.

"Oww!" Martin cried, gently pushing her away so she would see his wound.

"Oh, sorry," Coretta apologized, this time easing her left arm around him and kissing him gently on his right side only. "Are you okay?" She asked, tightening her grip. She began to cry, unaware she was crushing the white carnations she had purchased at the Atlanta airport while waiting for her flight. There were five flowers, representing her and each of their four children.

The doctor turned various shades of red as he watched the Kings passionately kissing. He was standing very close to them and was temporarily tied to the scene by the roll of gauze tape he held in his hand. The other end of the tape roll was wrapped around Dr. King's shoulder. Turning his head away, the doctor smiled.

Once she heard her husband's voice, Coretta had become oblivious to the presence of any one else in the room. Martin meaningfully cleared his throat. Coretta responded, immediately. Turning, she faced the onlookers. Fidgeting with her hands and blushing, Coretta could only maintain eye contact with the others for a fraction of a second. Dr. King placed his right arm around his wife, looked deeply into her eyes and said, "It's only a flesh wound. The bullet just barely grazed my shoulder. I'll be all right."

Mrs. King said nothing. After a short silence Martin announced, without taking his eyes off his wife, "All right, everybody out! I want to be alone with my wife." Without protest, everyone except the doctor, started filing out of the packed motel room.

Ralph pointed to the wall, saying, "We'll be right next door," stuttering slightly.

The doctor continued wrapping Martin's injured shoulder. "That means you, too, Doc. I think we can handle it from here," Martin explained.

"But I'm not quite finished, " the doctor replied.

"Oh yes, you are," Don, the big rhino-man uttered, in a deep voice. Putting his massive arms around the doctor's waist and lifting him with ease, Don carried the doctor out of the room. The gauze roll fell from the doctor's grasp and rolled harmlessly on the floor. At the other end, some of the blood-stained wrapping unraveled off Dr. King's shoulder.

As the doctor was being removed, he scooped up his small black leather bag off a table. Anxiously, he reached into the bag and quickly removed a small bottle of pills, holding them up, as if doing a commercial. "At least let me give you something for the pain," he said hurriedly before he was carried out the hotel room.

Looking into the eyes of his beautiful wife, Martin answered, "I have everything I need for the pain." There was a dull thud when the back of the doctor's head hit the top of the doorframe. The pills fell to the floor, rattling as they rolled under the bed. Don never stopped, slowed down, or looked back. The loyal, trusted servant merely closed the door and locked it behind him.

Coretta, who was fighting very hard to hold her laughter inside until after the door was closed, looked at her husband and remarked, "Maybe *he* should take something for the pain."

They were finally alone. Martin and Coretta met in a long passionate embrace. He told her he loved her and thanked God continuously that she was his wife. When they finally broke their embrace, Coretta picked up the gauze roll and began to complete the task the doctor had started.

"Martin, when is this ever going to stop? The obscene phone calls, the death threats – I just can't take it anymore. How many more times will you be beaten, spat on and thrown into jail? How many more near misses will there be? Sakes alive, I didn't even get a phone call this time. I heard a news bulletin on television. I caught the first thing smoking so I could get here as quickly as possible. Actually, the plane from Atlanta was booked solid, but I guess when they found out who I was they took pity on me."

Coretta cupped her hands on her face, temporarily damming the steady flow of tears that had started to race down her face. "I'm tired," she sobbed through her tears. "Martin, I'm so tired."

Though Mrs. King very much understood the importance of her husband's work and the dangers involved, every few months Martin had to reassure her. He would lovingly explain the importance of the mission. He had done this repeatedly, knowing it was what Coretta needed.

Martin embraced his wife once more, saying, "Be strong, my love. This won't be happening much longer. I've got this feeling."

Coretta looked up at her husband, again. Her eyes were as red as rubies and as wet as rain. "I'm sorry, Martin. Please forgive me," she said. "I just don't want anything to happen to you."

"I love you, too," Martin answered, then he continued, "Hey, I haven't seen you in weeks. It's very unfortunate it took something of this magnitude to reunite us. But God knows exactly what he is doing. Let's spend this time together, just the two of us. No strikes. No rallies. No freedom marches. No kids . . . , just us!"

Martin held his wife's face in his hands and used his thumbs to wipe her tears away. Reaching up, Coretta covered Martin's hands with her hands.

Wanting to feel as much pleasure as possible from her husband's caress, Coretta closed her eyes. She felt the soothing warmth of his hands on her hands and face increase when he said, "I think there is some wine in the refrigerator."

They sipped wine and talked for hours about the past, present and future. It was as if they had not seen or talked to each other for years. With their heads embedded upon a pillow, and holding hands, Martin and Coretta lay in bed looking toward the ceiling as though there was a television mounted there. As time passed, wine disappeared. Martin and Coretta were at the point where they were attempting to drink from the wine glasses without raising their heads from the pillows. A giggle from Coretta and a heavy bass laugh from Martin would surface with each failed attempt.

There was a warm and happy silence, like that of sitting in front of a fireplace on a winter evening with a loved one. Then, Martin turned toward his wife, as if he had heard a tear roll down her face. When he looked, he saw what was once a large tear slowly decrease in size as it left a trail from the corner of Coretta's eye to her ear that even a blind detective could follow. "What's wrong?" Martin inquired.

Coretta was slightly startled by her husband's voice. "Oh, oh, nothing, I was just thinking about the first poem you wrote to me," she answered.

"Was it that bad?" Martin asked, a hint of amusement behind his words.

Coretta smiled, saying, "No, Silly. It made me very happy. It was when we were first dating." The expression on her face changed slightly. "Do you remember it?" she quizzed.

"Do I remember? Do I remember? Do I remember?" Martin said, opening his arms and raising them toward the ceiling as if to ask God, "Why is she asking me something so simple?" He continued, "Of course I remember. The first gift I ever gave you was a scripture—Philippians 1:3-6, which I typed out and mounted in a frame. But inside of the frame, behind the scripture page, was a poem inside an envelope. Clever, huh? You had it for months and didn't know it was inside the frame. On the night I asked you to go steady, I pulled it out and read it to you. I will never forget the look on your face."

Martin and Coretta turned toward each other. They lay there, looking into each other's eyes. "Of course, I remember the poem . . . ," Martin said as he began to recite it to Coretta just like he had the first time.

One Day You Will Know . . .

One day you will know how much I love you . . .
one day you will know how much I care
to tell you these things now I wouldn't dare
these words that I speak are so very true
although, only in God's time
will they become due

One day you will know how much I begged God
that of my life you would some day be a part
oh . . . the long tearful prayers
oh . . . the two a.m. walks
in the early morning air
that is when I begged God
for a love so strong and true
I fasted, fasted, and prayed
that it would be you

One day you will know that I think

you are beautiful inside and out
when it comes to faith in God
I am one who will never doubt
so I hope and pray and I hope and I pray
that we will be together one beautiful day

One day you will know
that I seek you with all my heart
although at the same time
that very thing is being torn apart

My heart grieves because I love you so
yet if there is love from you I do not know
I can't help that I care so much
although I yearn with arduous patience
for your tender touch
not the touch from skin to skin
but rather, the touching
from souls within

however until the day 'that you will know'
I pray that our relationship continues to grow
these deep caring feelings
for you will never end
so I pray fervently that you will
open your heart and let me in

Coretta . . . one day you will know

"Didn't think I remembered, did you?" Martin asked. Coretta didn't bother to answer. Instead, she rolled onto her back, fluffed her pillow and waited, only for a second, to exhale.

"Wow," she said. Her mind now began to swim, not because of the wine. But, partly because the words the man whom she loved with all her heart had just spoken to her, but mainly because of the fact he had remembered it after all those years.

"Now let me ask you something," requested Martin. "Do you remember the first song I wrote and sang to you?"

Coretta instantly raised her open arms and hands toward the ceiling and said. "Do I remember? Do I remember? Do I remember? Of course, I do!"

Martin got up and walked over to a guitar that had been propped in the corner of the room. He removed the cover and walked back toward his wife. Although he always did, he definitely had her full attention then. In the style of Bill Withers, he began to strum the wooden instrument. Immediately recognizing the tune, Coretta blushed. Her heart began to pump rhythmic sure beats. Unlike ever before in her life, she was beginning to experience the warmth of love. Martin began to sing...

It's 12:30 in the morning
just going to bed from a challenging day
ready to fall asleep
but first, on my knees to pray
I pray for my daily struggles
my church and my family
I pray for a loving world
as one day it can be

I say amen then lay down
for a night of peaceful bliss
then thoughts of her warm smile
her heart and joyful laugh
convince me that her I truly miss

Then back on my knees again to finish
a prayer that was never really done
but, now I beg God for a favor
nothing big, just a small one

Though she probably is asleep
and dreaming of pleasant things
God please interrupt her dreams
and tell her these words that I sing

I want you to tell her that I love her
I want you to tell her that I care
I want you to tell her that I miss her
because she's part of my life

I want you to tell her that I love her
I want you to tell her that I care
I want you to tell her that I miss her
and that one day she'll be my wife

I pause my prayers
to think of her once again
as missing her is always overwhelming
her love for God, I love so much
but for her, her zeal, her joy,
and her love are never enough
her beauty, at a level
at which most don't compare
is the beauty of God
which she shines everywhere

now I love and I miss her more than before
the void and hurt now expands past

where my heart has already tore

Salty tears upon my lips
that moments before rode my face
and I know the only way to relieve
this unbearable pain
is to continue to pray

So while I do...

I want you to tell her that I love her
I want you to tell her that I care
I want you to tell her that I miss her
because she's part of my life

I want you to tell her that I love her
I want you to tell her that I care
I want you to tell her that I miss her
and that one day she'll be my wife

When Martin ended the song, he laid the guitar down gently, never taking his eyes off his beautiful bride. He often referred to her, even after years of marriage, as his bride. He walked toward the bed Coretta lay upon. She rose to her knees and met him with a warm and tight hug. They embraced for a few seconds, until Martin gently picked his bride off the bed. He held her in his arms, saying, "I love you." Even with his wound, but grimacing slightly, he laid her gently onto the bed, as if she had the weight of a feather and the worth of gold. First, he hovered above her, supporting most of his weight on his elbows. Then, he lay upon her and kissed her passionately.

Out of the darkness of the nearly twilight room, there were only sounds of togetherness and breathing. Martin and Coretta lost track of all time as they made passionate love until sunrise. It was as if Martin poured himself into a cup of love he felt for his wife and the love in which they were making. And when Martin poured himself into that cup of love, Coretta responded by drinking from it.

Like its preceding day, April 5th was cold. Unlike the preceding day the sun was shining brightly. The warm sunlight commanded the red, yellow and white tulips, planted in front of the Lorraine Motel, to stand at full attention and salute while leaning in an easterly direction.

Although the curtains were drawn, the early sunrise kept no secrets from Room 306, as it found a way to penetrate the room, letting them know another day with new opportunities has come. Lying behind his wife, Martin cradled her close to him. He spoke gently and directly into her ear. Coretta turned to face her husband. They talked and cried together for about thirty minutes. Then, fatigue from being up most of the night began to take over.

Coretta laid her head on Martin's shoulder. "Owww!" the deep bass voice cried out in pain

"Oh, I'm sorry, Baby," Coretta responded, lifting herself off Martin's bandaged bullet wound.

"That's all right, Dear," Martin said, his voice quivering, slightly.

"Did you happen to see where that bottle of pain pills rolled?"

CHAPTER 14

"Come in. We're dressed," Dr. King said, *speaking up so his voice* could be heard through the wooden motel door. Ralph Abernathy, Julian and Cliff stepped into the small hotel room. Dr. King shivered slightly in the cold morning air. He caught a glimpse of Don and two other men, as Cliff closed the door. Knowing Ralph, Dr. King guessed at least two of them had been there on guard all night.

"We are ready, Ralph," said Dr. King. "Have a man escort Mrs. King to the airport."

Turning toward his wife, Dr. King said, "I love you. Hurry home so you can take care of the kids. Tell them I love them and miss them. I prayed that you wouldn't have to go through this much longer."

Coretta smiled. Then Martin sealed their good-byes with a kiss. She handed him one of the white carnations she had brought the night before. With that, she turned and walked toward the door. Looking back only once before shutting the door behind her, she said, "I love you too, Baby."

"Okay men, let's go. We have a schedule to keep. Let us not commit the sin of turning our backs on time," Dr. King said.

Reverend Abernathy and Cliff were the first to leave the motel room. Abernathy pulled his overcoat tighter, though he made sure he had not forgotten his sweater again. Julian followed right behind Cliff, but halted when Dr. King grabbed the inside of his elbow, pulling him aside. "Give us a second gentlemen. We'll be right out," Dr. King said.

Pausing and peering past the door to make sure no one was listening, he said in a low voice, "I don't know exactly who you are, but I do know who you are not. You see, I called the *Detroit News* . . . ," Dr. King paused. Reading the changing of expressions on Julian's face, he continued, "But I do know where you come from or should I say when?"

"Does he really know or is he bluffing? No, he can't be bluffing," Julian thought. But he answered, "How and when did you find out?"

Dr. King continued. "Don't worry. Your secret is safe with me. Just do me one favor. When you go back, remember that God has a destiny planned for each and every one of us. You can't change your own destiny. Even God's Son was destined to die on the cross, as it was written for Judas to perish for betraying Him. But, I will give you this: though you can't change your own destiny, you can help create someone else's.

Standing face to face with Dr. King, Julian was at a loss for words. Handing Julian the white carnation his wife had given him, Dr. King said, "Here, give this to someone you love." He patted Julian on the back and ushered him through the doorway. Pulling the door shut, he then stepped out onto the balcony.

Julian, Cliff and Dr. King's staff completely surrounded him. There was a crunching sound of marching steps as the civil rights leaders and their entourage walked along the balcony. When they had walked about fifteen feet, this time, Dr. King stopped suddenly.

Sidestepping the man who was behind him, Dr. King turned and headed back toward Room 306, uttering, "Oh, I forgot my brief case." The entire group was totally caught by surprise as Dr. King easily separated himself from them.

Meanwhile, down below, the car carrying Mrs. King to the airport was just leaving the Lorraine Motel parking lot. The driver turned out of the south driveway, turned right onto Butler Street, and then turned right at Mulberry Street. Coretta faced the motel. She gazed out of the window as the cautious driver slowly picked up speed.

She spotted the group of civil rights leaders on the balcony, but in the midst of black overcoats, she could not locate the man she loved. Then she saw Martin dart back toward the hotel room. Coretta smiled, thinking, "Oh, he is so forgetful. He would forget his head if it weren't attached."

Her attention was diverted as she saw a twinkle of light coming from the bushes that separated the swimming pool from the parking lot. Her expression changed from a look of love to one of concern. Then it changed to a look of sheer terror.

"No, no, nooooo!" Her sounds of alarm and terror were wasted. They were muffled sounds to all but Coretta and the driver, as the screams were absorbed into interior of the closed car like water into a dry sponge.

Once again, what sounded like the sound of a very loud firecracker filled the air. It was the second time in as many days Julian had heard that noise. It was also the second time in as many days his heart had plummeted to his feet because of it.

Dr. King collapsed on the balcony once again. It was as if the day before had been a dress rehearsal. However, this time Julian was sprayed with blood from head to foot. Security by the police was light; supposedly, they had the lone gunman from the previous day in jail. As it turned out, security was lax enough to allow another gunman to lurk in the bushes. Dr. Martin Luther King, Jr. died on that cold day of April 5, 1968.

CHAPTER 15
The End and The Beginning

The Time Team was devastated. They witnessed a great man's life horribly and brutally taken right before their eyes. This man arguably was the most important man in America's civil rights history. Even Agent Pugh, who was superficially elated, because technically he had completed the most important part of his mission, felt heavy remorse.

Later that evening, in the 21st century, Julian was relaxing at his home in his favorite leather recliner. He was mentally and physically spent. He had remarked several times he would want to die in that chair. Sharing the same chair, Jasmine curled next to Julian, welcoming him home.

They had just finished eating dinner and were sipping wine as they watched the evening news. Jasmine, who wasn't paying much attention to the broadcast, twirled a single flower using a thumb and index finger. Smelling it, she smiled. She didn't know this flower was the same white carnation Dr. King had given to Julian only seconds before to his death.

Julian's thoughts were also somewhere else. He was thinking of the failed mission, but not so much of the events. He was transfixed on the statement Dr. King had made to him shortly before he was assassinated, the remark about not being able to change a person's destiny but being able to help create a person's destiny. Julian wondered, was it destiny that Time Team go back in time and interact with the past so they could all be changed. Everyone on the Time Team had changed in some way. Julian loved his wife more. Ricochet, one that would probably never truly fall in love, was now in love with Kat. And, even Ham and Bill were good friends now. "If those two are good friends then anything his possible," Julian thought, "Is it our destiny to do it again?"

The news shifted to a story about the candidates for the upcoming presidential campaign. It highlighted the candidates from the newly formed third party, the Liberation Party. The candidates were Senator Gregory O'Neal King and Colin Powell. They were running for the presidency and vice presidency of the United States, respectively.

Senator King responded to the interviewer's questions.

" . . . . Yes, I do realize if I am voted in as this great nation's President, I will indeed become the youngest man in history to ever hold that office. I was always the youngest in everything I was involved in. I was the youngest of five children. I was also always the youngest in my classes in school, so I am used to it. However, I think my years in the Senate and negotiations abroad while serving as Secretary of State for this great nation more than make up for any experience my opponents claim I lack. Furthermore, I am not ashamed to openly say I want to become the first African-American to hold the office of President of the United States."

Senator King had always been a strong man and a strong leader. However, he began to cry during the interview when the questions became personal. But Senator King's tears were the result of an overflow of emotions as he talked about his father. He continued, "My father, Dr. Martin Luther King, Jr. was a great man. Although I never got the chance to meet him, I have always known him very well, because he has been inside me," clinching his fist and bringing it in a sideways motion toward the center of his chest.

Julian's mouth hung open as he listened to the news interview. When it was over he looked at his wife with a puzzled expression. He asked her what was going on, explaining to her Dr. King had only four children.

"Where have you been for the last thirty years, Julian? Dr. Martin Luther King, Jr. had five children," Jasmine explained. "He only had four children when he was assassinated on the fifth of April in 1968. However, his wife, Coretta, was pregnant with their fifth child when he was killed. Some historians theorize Mrs. King became pregnant with Senator King only hours before her husband's death."

Julian began to weep tears of joy. When he first returned from the mission, he had only told Jasmine they had failed at their attempt to save Dr. King. But now he felt he should tell her everything about how the Time Team had apparently altered the future. Julian shared with his wife what Dr. King had said to him concerning God and destiny.

After sharing everything with Jasmine, Julian held her. Looking deeply into her eyes, he said, "I now believe in God and Jesus Christ." Without taking his eyes off her, he spoke directly to the computer saying, "Computer, locate Dr. Bill Rousseau."

After a brief second, the computer responded, "Dr. Rousseau is at the Greater Detroit Discipling Church. Would you like me to contact him?"

"Yes! By all means!" Julian answered. Once they were connected, Julian said a few words to Bill before hanging up. He never took his eyes off his wife, nor did she take her eyes off him. He spoke again. Only this time it was directed toward his wife. "Let's go."

It was Wednesday night and midweek service was already in session when Julian and Jasmine walked into the church. Julian was surprised to see the rest of the Time Team there. Bill had invited them.

Taking Julian into a secluded room, Bill and some other members of the church studied the Bible for several hours.

When it was time, Bill and another Christian brother led Julian into the water. Bill asked Julian two questions. He said, "Do you believe Jesus died and was resurrected on the third day?"

Julian replied, "Yes, yes I most certainly do."

Bill continued. "What then, is your good confession?"

Without hesitating Julian replied exuberantly, "Jesus is Lord!"

Then in the name of the Father, the Son and the Holy Spirit, they baptized Julian into the Kingdom of God.

The end of the story for you

The beginning of life for Julian

About the Author

Jean-Claude Lewis, born in Detroit, Michigan, left at the age of 19 to join the U.S. Navy and pursue a career as a Nuclear Engineer. He served onboard two nuclear submarines, allowing him to travel nearly the entire world. This gave him, for the next ten years, a life that was one hundred times greater in danger, adventure, and drama than   that of Huckleberry Finn's on the Mississippi River. On December10, 1995, he became saved and embarked upon a new and more exciting life.